Ab(

Sylvia Weiss Sinclair is one of the first baby boomers born in Los Angeles, California. When Sylvia was a child, from time to time, her mother, who was raised in southern Alabama, took her and her two brothers to visit their grandparents' farm. At fourteen years of age, Sylvia took the train on her own to Alabama in the summer of 1960 and started journaling her observations and experiences. She has earned an Associate Degree in Chemistry, a Bachelor of Arts in Business, and a Teaching Certificate for Secondary Education. She now lives in Bay Minette, Alabama, close to her mother's family. She is a member of the Alabama Writers' Forum and the Alabama Writers' Cooperative. She also leads a writers' group in Bay Minette, Alabama. She published *Roomie-Zoomies Forever* in the Birmingham Arts Journal. Her first novel, *Fledermama's Son* was published in 2017. Her second novel, *Making Raisins Dance*, was published in 2018. She has also published a short story, *Granny's Ghost*, in the anthology, *These Haunted Hills, Volume 2* in 2020.

THE GHOSTS OF DYAS CREEK

Sylvia Weiss Sinclair

THE GHOSTS OF DYAS CREEK

Vanguard Press

VANGUARD PAPERBACK

© Copyright 2021
Sylvia Weiss Sinclair

A CIP catalogue record for this title is
available from the British Library.

ISBN 978-1-80016-003-3

*Vanguard Press is an imprint of
Pegasus Elliot MacKenzie Publishers Ltd.*
www.pegasuspublishers.com

First Published in 2021

**Vanguard Press
Sheraton House Castle Park
Cambridge England**

Printed & Bound in Great Britain

Dedication

This book is dedicated to my remarkable mother, Dorothy Margaret Pimperl Weiss (1916 – 2007), who told me stories of her life.

Acknowledgements

I have to start by thanking my husband, Mike Sinclair and my brother, Norman Weiss, for reading and editing my final manuscript. This book would not have been possible without their support and encouragement. It has truly been a surreal process.

I would like to express my many thanks to all the literary ladies in the Bay Minette Writers Group, especially Mary, Sharon, Chell, and Loretta, for reading my early drafts, offering advice, and keeping me focused.

A big thank you to Suzanne Mulvey, commissioning editor of Pegasus Mackenzie Elliot Publishers Ltd., who saw the value of my manuscript and offered to publish it.

Also, many thanks to my Uncle Paul, who told me the details of the ghost story my Grandmother Margaret once told so long ago. A special thanks to Van Johnson, who shared his memories of growing up in the south. And thanks to Dewitt Roley, Frank

Klasnich, who knew my grandparents and their seven children, years ago.

I interviewed many locals, who grew up in the south to hear their point of view of the race relations they experienced. In my opinion, most people outside of Alabama tend to stereotype Alabama like it was decades ago. Alabama has changed over the years with the civil rights movement and the influence of Martin Luther King Jr.

I have based my book on a true story and used the names of actual locations, and the characters who have since passed on to eternity. But I have changed the names and characterizations of people living, to classify as a work of fiction. In addition, I have listened closely to the ladies in my quilting group and my church group to replicate the 'southern accent' in the dialogue.

PART 1

CHAPTER 1

Deep in the south Alabama woods, where the longleaf pines stretch to the azure sky, Margaret waddles out of the old wooden farmhouse and looks up at the thousands of sparkling stars in the clearing between the towering pines. The full moon is rising in the eastern sky, casting shadows in a clearing of the thick wooded wilderness.

John calls after her, "Margaret, can't you wait until morning to feed leftover scraps to the pigs in the barn?"

"No, John, I don't like the garbage stinking up the house. Besides, the smell of it brings vermin," Margaret insists, turning her head to see John standing in the doorway. "I will not raise my children in a house full of filthy rats running about."

Margaret, barely five-foot-tall, but as round as a ripe pumpkin, is eight months pregnant with her fifth child. Her towering six-foot-tall husband, John, tries to detain her, but Margaret loves the cool night air, the sweet smell of the pines and the starry night sky. She hears the night sounds of frogs and insects chirping out their songs. She thinks how different this remote area is to the big city of Chicago, where her sister, Ella, lives.

While walking to the newly built barn where they keep pigs, chickens and a milking cow, Margaret sees something ghostly and mysterious moving in the forest.

At first, she thinks it is just the moon passing behind a cloud in the sky, throwing shadows between the trees. Then something seems to be coming slowly closer and closer to Margaret. Out of the tall pines, a form takes on the shape of an old man with a long white beard wearing a flowing white shroud. His skin appears to be burnt and rotting off the bones. His eyes are missing, leaving only hollow orbs in his skull. His bony hands reach out to Margaret, beckoning her to come closer.

Margaret screams… Faints.

Falling to the ground, she hits her head on a sharp rock. Her blue gingham skirt spreads out around her like a fan as she lays unconscious.

John and the four small children run out of the farmhouse towards the scream. John is still in his overalls and work boots from the day in the fields and the four girls in cotton calico summer dresses, all barefooted on that hot humid night.

"Mama, Mama," Dotty, the eldest, cries out in her high-pitched voice.

"Margaret? Can you hear me? What happened? Are you…" John yells, but Margaret doesn't make a sound. Swiftly John sweeps her up into his arms. Softly, he brushes his hand across Margaret's brow, feeling the flush of fever. Then he carries her back to the farmhouse, the four daughters trailing behind. In the bedroom, John gently lays Margaret on the quilted flowered bedspread of their four-poster bed. She is bleeding slightly from the back of her head, staining the pillow her head rests upon, matting her long brown hair.

The four young girls cluster around their mother on the bed, shaking with fear. John turns to the oldest girl and says, "Dotty, run… Go tell Mr. Ryan your mother is hurt. May need the doctor in town. Quick!"

In a flash, Dotty takes off, running down the dirt road, tall pines on either side, her bare feet slapping against the soft red clay, leaving their print. She can run so fast her sisters call her "Horsy Dotty". Even though the Ryan family lives two miles away, Dotty is on their doorstep in thirty minutes, knocking on their wooden door.

"Who is it?" Jim Ryan says, swinging the front door wide open. He sees Dotty Pimperl huffing to catch her breath. "Dotty! What is it? What happened?"

"It's Mama, Mr. Ryan. She's hurt. Papa said to come get you. Quick!"

"Annie!" Jim yells to his wife. "Margaret's hurt. May need some doctorin'. I'm goin' to see what I can do. Lil' Dotty's here to get me. We'll take the Model T."

"God's speed, Jim. I'll be prayin' for y'all," Annie calls back.

Mr. Ryan and Dotty run out to the barn where Jim's prize motorcar sits, waiting for an emergency such as this. Jim puts his hand to the crank and starts turning over the engine. The motorcar balks at Jim as he begins to crank and backfires like the sound of a shotgun.

Stinky black fumes bellow out of the tailpipe. A few more cranks and it shakes violently and then rumbles to life.

Soon the motor is humming, and the two passengers climb into the front leather seat. Putting it into gear, the car backfires again, then the car slowly moves forward out of the barn. Another shift of the gears and they are on their way.

Chapter 2

On the way to the Pimperl's farmhouse, Jim Ryan thinks back to 1910 when he first met his friends, John Pimperl and Sam Sandberg. The three of them were working at the Blackstone, a posh hotel on the banks of Lake Michigan in Chicago. John worked as a bartender and Jim, a waiter in the banquet room. Sam worked in the kitchen, chopping and prepping the food for the cooks. All three immigrated through Ellis Island. Jim Ryan was a tall, lanky Irishman, with a shock of red hair and a taste for whiskey. Sam Sandberg was a stocky fair-haired Swede who enjoyed a dark stout brew.

After work, Jim and Sam hung out with John at the bar and talked of their future in America. One day Albert Huff, a cantankerous old German, who worked at the *Chicago Tribune*, came in and sat down at the bar. Huff had heard of an abandoned farm in lower Alabama that was to be auctioned off for back taxes. Huff was looking for investors, and both Jim Ryan and Sam Sandberg jumped at the chance to buy a piece of land. Jim remembers Sam saying with a laugh, "We should go for it, Jim. They are not making any more land here." The three men speculated it would be a good investment and bought the farm. As time went by, Huff argued the property was too far away and he could never make any money on it. That's when John Pimperl, a farmer from the fertile mountains of Austria, offered to buy Huff's share of the farmland. Pimperl did not have enough money to buy Huff outright, but Huff took a note for the balance and every month John Pimperl paid toward the balance of the note.

The three immigrants, Ryan, Sandberg and Pimperl, put their heads together and decided to move down to Alabama all together and set up farming. By 1920, the three men and their families were ready for the great adventure, but John Pimperl's wife, Margaret was not. She was pregnant again. She already had two little girls, Dotty, four years old and Helen, two. Margaret immigrated from Budapest, Hungary and loved city life, but her husband, John, did not. He longed to put his hands in the soil, to plant and grow his own food.

It was a long trip on the train from Chicago to the southern part of Alabama. In coach, the rows of worn leather seats were filled with immigrants from southern and eastern Europe, looking to farm the rich black soil of Alabama. Also traveling in coach were freed slaves, whose ancestors moved north after the Civil War to find work in the big cities like Detroit, Chicago, and Cleveland. However, when the train crossed over the Mason-Dixon Line, the train came to a stop. The conductor then rounded up all the colored people and moved them to the last coach car of the train.

In Mobile, the three men pooled their money and bought several mules, wagons, tools, seed and provisions. They hooked up the mules to the wagons, loaded up and headed northeast to the remote farmland next to Dyas Creek.

In the woods, they found the old wooden farmhouse with many rooms. The men cut down some of the tall pine trees nearby with a long bowsaw and stripped off the branches. Then they went about cutting the farmhouse into three pieces. Raising one end of the farmhouse, they positioned one of the logs underneath and hooked two mules to the house, pulling it away to the land nearby. Slowly, a portion of the house rolled on the enormous log as another log was placed beneath the house. The three men labored for days, moving two of the three pieces to other parts of the land. Then the men worked together to rebuild the houses to completion and helped each other build barns for the mules and farming equipment.

It was a hard life for Margaret. She gave birth to her third girl, Elizabeth, shortly after their arrival in 1920. Two years later, Anitha was born in the old rubber bathtub, like her sister, with the help of a midwife.

Chapter 3

As Jim Ryan and Dotty roll down the dusty dirt road to the Pimperl homestead, black clouds crowd out the stars and the sky grows dark. A flash of lightning lights up the murky sky, then a crash of thunder. Again, and again the sky lights up with streaks of lightning, like fireworks on the fourth of July, and thunder rumbles through the night. Now the heavens break open, and rain comes down faster than the wipers can clear the windshield. The dusty roads turn into rivers of mud. The tires start spinning then dig their way down into the muck. Mr. Ryan gets out of his motorcar in the pouring rain. He tries to push the sunken car out of the mudhole, but he is stuck. Slipping and sliding, he sees it is useless to escape from the mire that holds his car captive.

"Dotty, we're stuck. Let's just get out and make a run for it. I can see the lanterns burning inside the farmhouse from here."

"Okay, Mr. Ryan. If you say so."

With the rain pouring down, they slosh through the muddy road in the dark toward the brightly lit farmhouse like moths to a flame.

***

As they approach the farmhouse, Dotty thinks back to when they first arrived at the farm in Alabama close to Dyas Creek. She remembers how hard life was for her mother, Margaret. There was no running water. Every other day, she helped her mother pile the baby's cloth diapers into a wheel barrel and roll it down to the spring. There, they dug out the sand until the spring flowed with clean water. In a large black caldron close to the spring, Margaret and Dotty filled it with diapers and spring water, then built a fire under the pot and boiled the diapers until they were clean and sterile. Eventually her father, John, built a pump close to the farmhouse and erected a metal windmill to pump the water out of the ground. Dotty remembers her mother crying every day from the hardships of living out in the Alabama woods and missing the conveniences of the big city.

***

Reaching the steps of Dotty's home, soaked to the skin, shivering, they rush up to the porch, where John is waiting in the open doorway.

"Quick, Jim and Dotty, come inside. Here, wrap these blankets around you so you don't catch your death," John says, handing each a woolen blanket.

"How's Margaret, John? What happened?" Jim asks.

"I'm not sure. She went out to the barn to feed the pigs some slop and then we heard her scream. We found her passed out on the ground, with her head oozin' blood. I told her not to go out at night, wait 'til morning, being she's awful clumsy, carrying that baby and all. It's due soon, ya' know, maybe in a few weeks. But she wouldn't listen," John says, looking down at the floor. He feels the ache of remorse, bringing Margaret way out here in the middle of nowhere, miles and miles from civilization.

"Now, now, John. Ya know how independent and stubborn she is. Don't blame yourself. She'll be okay," Jim says, placing a hand on his shoulder, as he tries to comfort his long-time friend.

"Oh, my head," Margaret moans in the other room. The two men have been talking, just outside the bedroom, as Margaret awakens. She reaches up with her open palm to where her head aches and feels a large knot on the back of her head. The bleeding has stopped now, but she feels something is terribly wrong. The baby inside her is not moving around like before. She is afraid to say anything, fearing for the health of her baby she has carried for eight long months.

"Oh, thank God. She's coming around." John breathes a sigh of relief. What would he do without Margaret? How would he take care of the four girls and all the farm work? And the baby on the way, is it going to be okay?

The horrible sight she saw in the woods will not leave her mind. She calls out to her husband, "John. John, where are you?"

John rushes into the bedroom, with Jim Ryan right behind him. "Margaret! Thank God you're all right. What is it, Margaret?"

Margaret sits straight up in her feather down bed and looks wide eyed at John. She barely gets the words out. In a shaky voice she says, "Old man Gelsinger... I... I saw him."

"Gelsinger? Old man Gelsinger has been dead for two years."

"I know, I know, John. But I saw him coming out of the woods. He was just a shadow, but I recognized that long white beard. He was reaching out to me. Trying to tell me something."

CHAPTER 4

Besides the Ryan family and the Sandberg family, the Pimperl family had another neighbor who lived deep in the woods, a rugged old alligator hunter, by the name of Gelsinger. He was tall and wiry, with wrinkled, weathered skin and a long white beard. He claimed to be Rumanian, but some folks thought he could be part native American by the way he lived off the land. He built his one room shack out of rough sawn timber at the edge of the piney woods next to the farmland John Pimperl settled on.

Wearing only his coveralls and mud boots, the old man would go out on Dyas Creek in his fourteen-foot-long boat hunting for 'gators when the sun went down. From the glow of his lantern, he would look for the red eyes of the alligators floating just above the water.

"Them big old 'gators bring a right pretty price from them traders up in Mobile," Gelsinger would say. The traders back then sold the alligator skins to merchants in Chicago, who in turn made shoes, purses and other high-priced fashions. The old man would sell the skins and smoke the meat for alligator stew. He squirreled away the money he got for selling the skins, stuffing the coins and dollars in mason jars, then burying the jars under his house in a hole in the ground.

He kept the jars of money hidden from sight under some crushed tin cans, until he needed something in town like salt, coffee, and other staples. Everything else he could make, trap, or grow.

Gelsinger would ride his great white horse over to the Pimperl's homestead to drop off their mail or trade meat from a fresh kill, for Margaret's homemade biscuits and peach preserves. They were good neighbors and Gelsinger liked to sit on the Pimperl's screened in porch in the evening and tell stories of hunting alligators.

Once, while sitting in their old wooden rocking chair on the porch, Gelsinger fell asleep waiting for Margaret. She came out with her biscuits and canned peaches for the old man and saw him sleeping. She hated seeing his dirty old beard, smelling of leftover hash, hanging on his leathery old chin. She went back inside and got her scissors, then she cut the old man's beard clean off, leaving nothing but grey stubble.

When Gelsinger awoke, Margaret had left the biscuits and canned goods nearby the rocking chair. He reached down to get them but felt a draft on his face. He went to stroke his long beard, but it was gone. He was so mad, he let out a fierce shriek like a wounded bobcat. "What the heck! Ack! Margaret! Margaret, did you cut m' beard?"

"Why yes, Mr. Gelsinger. It stinks! It smells of all the food it catches plus the sinful tobacco you chew.

You think you spit it out, but that old beard of your'n catches most of it."

"Miss Margaret, you have no business cuttin' my beard. You keep them scissors away from me, ya hear?" And with that, the old man stomped off and ran back to the woods, leaving behind the fresh baked biscuits and the jar of sweet yellow peaches.

***

It was said that old man Gelsinger had thousands of dollars hidden away in mason jars. But he was content to live alone in the woods, drinking a little hooch he brewed from scuppernong grapes. The plump purple grapes grew wild on vines, tangled in the tree branches throughout the forest and around his shack.

One night after sundown, two men, Ronnie and Roy, came around to Gelsinger's shack. They had been drinking down at the tavern and heard a couple of loggers talking about all Gelsinger's money. The two men were down on their luck and thought robbing the old man, who lived all alone, would be an easy way to score some cash.

Ronnie and Roy had been friends for years since they dropped out of school at sixteen and hung out together. They worked odd jobs around town to earn money for beer.

Ronnie was real tall and skinny. His blue jeans hung loose on him and he always had a pack of cigarettes rolled up in the sleeve of his white tee shirt. He was a chain smoker and went through two packs a day. He wore his dirty blonde hair long enough to slick it back with his uncut fingernails. He was most proud of his cowboy boots made with alligator skin sewn on the top of the boot.

Roy was meatier than Ronnie and liked to chew tobacco. His blue jeans fit tight and he always tucked in his grey thermal shirt to look manlier. He wore a leather belt to hold up his pants, while his belly hung over his belt. His jet-black hair was cut short and greased with hair goo to make his hair stand straight up.

Standing in the dark, outside Gelsinger's shack, Roy put another pug of tobacco in his cheek and started to chew. Ronnie nervously pulled out a cigarette, tucking it behind his ear for later. They both stared at each other, waiting to say something. Ronnie spoke first. "Roy, how we goin' a do this?"

"Well," Roy started to speak then spat a stream of tobacco juice out of his mouth. "You knock on the door…"

"What? Why me? It's y… your… idea," Ronnie stuttered his reply.

"Hey, that's why you knock. I'm not doing everything myself. Now knock on the damn door!"

"Okay! Okay!" and Ronnie knocked on the door.

"Who's there?" Gelsinger said from inside the shack.

"Oh… a neighbor," Ronnie said in a voice higher than normal.

As soon as Gelsinger opened the door, Roy pulled out his gun and pointed it at the old man. "Give me your money or I'll shoot."

The stubborn old man would not give them one cent. Desperate for money, Roy shot the old man. They searched Gelsinger's house but could not find anything of value. Taking the lantern siting on the table, Roy threw it down on the floor, set fire to the house and ran out of the house with Ronnie close behind. The wooden shack burned down to the ground with old man Gelsinger still inside it.

***

Margaret takes a deep breath; she is pale as a corpse. Now her thoughts were coming back to her. "Seein' that ghost comin' around the back, reachin' for me, I was so scared I… I screamed. The next thing I remember, I'm in this bed, with this big lump on the back of my head." Gingerly she touches the swollen bump.

"Maybe old man Gelsinger was tryin' to tell you who killed him," interrupts Jim.

"Or maybe, where his money is buried," adds John. "Ya know, no kin could be found, so the land went to the state to be auctioned off. And ya know, we folks bought the farm and the land surrounding the farmhouse, including where old man Gelsinger once lived. My guess is that the old man's ghost was tryin' to tell Margaret where he buried his money."

"Makes sense to me. That old man sure liked Margaret's biscuits." Jim remarks.

"Ya know, my Margaret bakes up some mighty fine biscuits. Maybe you're right, Jim."

Chapter 5

As Margaret lays in bed, shooting pains attack her lower back and her uterus starts to contract, trying to push her baby out of her womb. She doubles up with pain and beads of perspiration form on her forehead, running down the sides of her face.

"Oh! Oh John, the baby's comin'. It's too soon. It can't be. Oh…" she moans. Her water breaks and floods the bed. The contractions go on all night and the day is dawning.

By morning, Margaret is still in contractions, but the baby just will not come. Something is wrong. Margaret is exhausted from pushing all night. She is fading fast. She lays limp as a rag between each contraction, wrenching her whole being.

John feels panic setting in and shouts, "Jim, go get Sadie Sandberg. Tell her she must come quick. The baby is coming early. We need her help." John tries to hide his emotions, fearing he will lose his precious Margaret and the baby on the way. He strokes Margaret's clammy forehead, trying to comfort her, whispering soothing words in her ear. "Sweet Margaret… darlin'… you goin' a be okay. We've sent for Sadie Sandberg to help you through this. Just hang on a little longer… hang on…"

The storm blows through and the dirt road dries up. Jim runs out to his motorcar and starts it up. The wheels start to turn and slowly, the car crawls out of the mud. He drives over to the Sandberg's homestead.

"Sam! Sadie! Margaret Pimperl's baby is on the way. She needs your help."

Sadie, a certified midwife, is shocked that the baby is so early. She grabs her medical bag and dashes out of the house. She and Jim climb into the model T and within an hour, Jim returns with Sadie.

Sadie is soon at Margaret's side in the bedroom, feeling Margaret's huge stomach.

"Hey, Margaret, how you doin?" Sadie says, trying to sound cheerful.

"Not... so... well, Sadie," Margaret says in a weak, shaky voice.

"Humm. It feels like the baby is breach. Let's see if I can turn the little fella around. Now, Margaret, hold on. This may hurt some."

Sadie scrubs her hands in a bowl of water, then with Margaret's knees up, she reaches between Margaret's legs, with one hand way up into her uterus. Feeling around, she tries to turn the baby around then notices something unusual. The cord is wrapped around the baby's neck and the helpless infant in Margaret's womb is not moving.

Margaret moans in agony from the pressure of Sadie's hand trying to turn the baby, but too weak to cry out. She knows in her heart; something is not right.

Silently, she offers a little prayer up to God. "O Almighty God and Father, who art ever ready to help…"

Worried, Sadie says nothing more, but simply removes the cord from around the baby's neck and gently guides it headfirst through the birth canal. Slowly she maneuvers the infant's head, then shoulders, through Margaret's body, ripping soft tissue around the opening.

Margaret screams out in pain. Finally, the infant is free, but it does not move. Sadie slaps the baby boy on the bottom, but it does not cry. She tries again and again, with no result. She lays the lifeless baby boy on a small blanket and wraps it tight.

Sadie's eyes fill with tears. Her voice breaks. "Margaret, sweetie, I'm sorry, he just didn't make it. He's with the angels now."

Margaret buries her face in the pillow to muffle her heart-wrenching sobs. Her first baby boy is stillborn.

John, by her side, grips her hand, fighting back his tears. "Margaret, darlin'…" not knowing what to say, just holds on to her hand.

Margaret looks up with tearstained eyes, and John envelops her in his strong arms, rocking her gently. "Margaret, darlin'… It's gonna be… all right. Now you rest, ya hear, Margaret. Don't you worry about a thing. Just rest and get better. I'll take care of the girls. I'm here for you."

Margaret sighs and collapses in John's arms.

Chapter 6

Summer turns to fall, and the days grow cooler, and trees change from green to reds, golds and yellows. Margaret physically recovers from the loss of her stillborn child, but her heart still aches. John and the girls are busy harvesting peaches and plums, way too many to eat. The sweet fruity smell of ripening bushels of fruit coaxes Margaret into the kitchen. She touches a fuzzy pink peach and pushes her thumb and forefinger gently, feeling it give way under pressure. Margaret mutters, "Maybe putting up preserves will help mend the hole in my heart I feel, when my newborn baby boy died that awful night. The night I saw the ghost and fainted." Now she loathes going outside at night, for fear of what may be lurking in the woods. She stays close to the house and will not go to the barn at night.

John gets word the freight train has dropped off a special cargo from Chicago. John jumps into his rusty red Ford pickup. He guns the motor and heads down the dusty dirt road toward Jim Ryan's house.

Jim is cutting hay to roll up for feed in the winter. He hears John's old truck backfiring a time or two, then sees the pickup coming down the road in a cloud of dust.

Stopping his John Deere tractor, Jim yells out, "Hey, John, what's up?"

"It's here! The piano my brother sent me down from Chicago. He just bought a baby grand for his casino and asked me if I wanted his old upright one. I said, 'I sure do!' Figure a little music in the house will brighten up Margaret's mood. She sure is sad she lost that little baby boy back in August. The freight dropped it off at the depot in town. Can ya help me load 'er up, Jim?"

"Sure can, John. Just have to let Annie know where we're goin'," Jim says, jumping down off his tractor to dash inside. Then out he comes and climbs into John's pickup and off they go.

At the depot, a five by five by two-foot wooden crate sits on the loading dock. John goes into the station to fill out the paperwork. When he comes out, Jim helps load it into the back of John's pickup and tie it down securely.

Down highway thirty-one they drive slowly, avoiding any bumps. Then, turning down the dirt road to the farmhouse, they hear the children playing out front. When the girls see the large wooden crate in the back of their papa's truck they squeal with delight. "What is it, Papa? What's in the big wooden box?"

Margaret, still in her apron from cooking, comes out of the house to see what all the commotion is about. "What in the world you got there, John?" she says, eyeing the back of his pickup.

"You will see, my lil' ol' sweet Margaret," he says, as Jim helps him unload the crate in front of the old farmhouse. "Jim, get the crowbar out of my tool chest in my truck." Slowly the two men pry the wooden boards apart, revealing a five-foot-tall, magnificent, dark mahogany, upright piano. The gold lettering above the keyboard reads, *Mathushek — New Haven, CT.*

Margaret's frown turns to shock then to surprise, seeing the piano. "Oh, my Lord! A real piano!" She rubs her eyes in disbelief. She nearly faints.

"Do ya like 'er, Margaret? It's for you," John says, opening the cover to show the ivory and ebony keys.

"Oh, my sweet Jesus! Do I like it? Such a question. Of course, John. How…"

"Margaret, my brother bought a new baby grand for his business in Chicago and asked me if I wanted it. He shipped it down here by freight, even paid the shipping. What do ya' think?" John knows Margaret's father taught her how to play the piano in his band in Budapest. She knows all the Hungarian tunes by heart.

"Oh John, it is wonderful. Let's get it in the house and I'll play you a tune," Margaret says excitedly, itching to finger the keyboard. With the help of Jim Ryan, they managed to maneuver the old piano into the living room. Margaret takes off her apron and uses it as a rag to wipe the dust off the shiny dark wood. Then she sits down in front of the piano and starts playing songs she knows from childhood.

Gyere Be Rose, gyere be.
Egyedül megyek.

35

Három cigány hegedül.
Gyere, érezd jól magad.

The children dance around the living room while the two men sit down to listen. John can see the color coming back in Margaret's cheeks, as she sings out to the melodies.

"Mama, Mama, it's so pretty. What does the song mean?" asks Dotty.

"Well, Dotty, it's an old gypsy tune. It goes:

Come in Rose, come in.
I'm walking by myself all alone.
Three gypsies are playing the violin.
Come enjoy yourself.

.

Dotty smiles and says, "Play it again, Mama. Play it again."

"Come on, Jim, I'll drive you back home," John says, glad to see Margaret smiling again.

"Okay, John. I better get back to mowing that hay." Then turning to Margaret, he says, "Now, Margaret, you just keep at that piano playing and we'll have a party next Saturday."

Margaret just smiles and plays a little waltz in the key of C in three-four time.

When John returns, he chases all the children out of the house. "Now, you children, go play outside in the sunshine. Go on, now. Papa and Mama need some alone time." The four girls go skipping out of the house humming some little tunes they heard their mother play.

He kisses Margaret on the back of the neck while she is playing *The Merry Widow's Waltz*, and she jumps up, startled, and says, "Oh, John!"

"How about a little romance, Margaret," John says with a wink.

"Oh, John," Margaret murmurs with a wink back. Playfully, she tries to escape. John chases her around the house until he catches her in the bedroom, and she surrenders to his passion.

Chapter 7

Over the next five years, Margaret gives birth to two more boys and John is thrilled to have the two boys help work the land. By the time the boys come along, John has corn, potatoes and peanuts growing every year. The hard work of breaking ground with a plow pulled by mules is over. John now has a John Deere tractor to work the soil, but there still is plenty of farm work for the boys. John also starts tapping the pine trees on his land for their sap. By cutting a chink in the trunk of a large pine tree and hanging a small bucket under the cut, as the sap rises in the trunk, some of the sap runs into the bucket. Once a week, John drives around and fills barrels in the back of his truck with the rich sap of the pine trees. When the barrels are full, John drives to town and sells the pine sap to the refineries in Mobile that convert it into turpentine and other industrial products. Tapping pine trees is easier work than farming and pays well.

As time goes on, John plants a grove of pecan trees. First, he plants the pecan nuts, then, as the seedlings grow thick enough, he grafts each one, using a branch from a mature producing tree from one of his neighbors.

When the pecan trees begin to bear nuts, Margaret gathers the pecans falling on the ground in November. She uses them for her coffee cakes and strudel.

Dotty is the first child in the family to start school in the one-room schoolhouse in Dyas. Every day she walks three miles down a dirt road through the pine forest to a clearing where a sawmill, hotel, general store, and restaurant stand near the red wooden schoolhouse. All grades, first through eighth, are taught by a tall, redheaded teacher named Miss Pepper. She teaches the three Rs: Reading, 'Riting' and 'Rithmetic'. Dotty easily learns reading and at six years old, tells her mother, Margaret, she will no longer speak German in the house, only English. Dotty adores Miss Pepper, but she has a temper to match her red hair. Nobody misbehaves in her classroom for fear of the dreaded hickory switch.

There are no black students in this little schoolhouse, only kids from the surrounding farms. The blacks live in another part of the town and have their own communities, including schools, churches, grocery stores and such. They didn't mix socially with the white folks. But farmers hire both black and white laborers to pick cotton, pecans, or other commodities in the fields. That is just the way it is in rural Alabama in the 1920s.

***

At fourteen, Dotty is blossoming into a long-legged young woman. Her mother, Margaret, bobs Dotty's dark auburn hair short, with bangs to her eyebrows, framing her sky-blue eyes.

Margaret is a no-nonsense mother, who does not want her daughters to be distracted by the farm boys in Alabama and end up pregnant, having babies with some no-account southerner, and having to marry at a young age. It is important for her girls to get an education past the third grade like herself. Dotty is plain enough, but she is already budding and soon the hormonal teenage boys will be noticing and want to romance her. If Margaret can keep Dotty busy until May, at least she will graduate.

Dotty loves school, especially reading. She reads *A Girl of the Limberlost*, a novel about a girl who collects moth larva and butterflies in jars. She watches the metamorphosis transform the larva into beautiful, winged insects. Then she sells them to a professor at a local college to earn money. Reading books takes her to realms beyond her humble home in the woods.

Dotty is also good at math. She can figure out problems like how much money will twenty bushels of corn bring in at sixty-nine cents a bushel. She learns much of her math from her father on the farm.

She is so good at math her mother and father include her in their weekly card game of bridge with Frank Huber. Huber, an old bachelor about John's age, lives in the back woods. He was an only child, who took care of his sickly parents all his life. When they both died of pneumonia one cold winter night, Frank took over the family farm. Living alone for years, he never took care of his hygiene such as brushing his teeth and washing himself or his clothes. But even though he is unkempt, John and Margaret invite him over for a game of bridge every week and Dotty sits in for a fourth.

As Dotty matures, Margaret notices Frank gawking at Dotty's chest during the bridge game. One evening, after the game, Frank corners John alone and asks, "Ya know John, your lil' ol' Dotty, sure would make me a mighty fine lil' ol' wife. I'd take real good care of her and you'd have one less mouth to feed."

John is shocked to hear Frank talk like that. His Margaret was twenty-five when they married, and he was twenty-eight. "Why, Frank, Dotty is just a child, barely fourteen years old, and you're more than twice her age."

"Oh, come on John, what she gonna do when she finishes school in May? You best marry her off before she gets too old and homely. You don't want her to be an ol' spinster like Miss Pepper at the schoolhouse," Frank says with a wink.

"Well, I'll have to talk it over with Margaret," John tells Frank, lowering his brow and cupping his hand over his mouth. "Now, Frank, I think you best be on your way home," he says, anticipating the argument with his wife over Frank's request.

Later that evening after all the children go to bed, John comes up to Margaret in the kitchen where she is tidying up and slips his arm around her waist. Then he tells her what Frank said to him about marrying Dotty.

"That stinky old man! How dare he say to you to give him our oldest daughter. Why, he just wants to get her to bear him children and work her in the fields from sunup to sundown. Lord, she is just a child! No. I won't have it! Don't you dare condemn her to such a hard life," Margaret says angrily, slamming her fist on the table, knocking over the salt and pepper shakers.

"Well Margaret, what... we gonna do? She has no other suitors."

Margaret sighs, realizing her options are limited. "I'll write my twin sister, Ella, in Chicago. Maybe she can get Dotty a job in the city."

That night, before Margaret goes to bed, she sits down at the kitchen table with pen and paper and writes a letter to her sister.

Dear Ella,
How are you? We are all fine here in this wooded wilderness called Alabama. I miss the city more than you will ever know. Days are getting shorter and soon Christmas will be here. Dotty just turned fourteen years old and will graduate from school in May. The only high school in these parts is in Mobile, fifty miles away. She's a good girl, but there are no opportunities for a young lady like Dotty. Do you think you can find her a job with

a good family? She is real good with children and she can clean house and wash laundry better than most. She has been a big help to me with all my other five children. Can you do me a favor and take Dotty under your wing?

Lots of love,

Your sister, Margaret

Chapter 8

In May, Dotty finishes the eighth grade and graduates from the Dyas Country School. Margaret's sister, Ella, sends Dotty a one-way train ticket from New Orleans to Chicago. Ella has a job lined up for Dotty as a domestic for a wealthy family. Ella knows all too well the hard life of a farmer's wife. From time to time, the rustic life on the farm, with all the cooking, cleaning and caring for six children and a husband, depresses Margaret. She takes to fits of crying and longs for the conveniences of electricity and indoor plumbing of the city. She writes to her sister, telling Ella of her hardships, and to *please* send her a train ticket to Chicago. On the train, Margaret can bring up to three children with her at no extra charge. So, she usually does.

Dotty cannot wait to get away from all the farm work of digging potatoes and shucking corn for the chickens. The best thing about school is getting out of chores. Now that school is over for her, she dreams of moving to the big city of Chicago. She packs her old carpet bag suitcase to the brim. Early Monday morning, John fires up the old Ford pickup and slings Dotty's suitcase into the bed of the pickup.

Margaret takes Dotty in her arms and whispers, "Now Dotty, those city boys may try to romance you and get the better of you. But don't you let them!" Margaret says sternly. "A man can shit in his hat and put it back on his head. But if a woman does it, she is dirty. You save yourself for a man who's respectful... and marries you... You hear, girl?"

"Yes, Mama. I will," Dotty says, looking down at her shoes, embarrassment showing in her reddening face. She never heard her mother talk that way to her, but she heeds the warning.

Dotty climbs in the cab next to her father. Margaret dabs the tears from her eyes with a well-worn lace hanky, watching her precious Dotty leave for the big city. Dotty's three sisters and two brothers stand on the steps of the wooden porch waving, shouting out goodbyes to their big sister.

It is a long trip to New Orleans, but they arrive by noon to check into the train station and find out the train leaves at twelve forty-five. Dotty and her father walk through the huge train station to the last train terminal, for train forty-eight, named *The City of New Orleans*. Standing in front of her assigned passenger car, Dotty gives her father one last hug as she holds back her salty tears.

John holds his daughter tight, not wanting to let go, and whispers in her ear, "Now Dotty, your Auntie Ella and Uncle Felix will meet you in the train station in Chicago at the end of the line. You be good, ya hear and work hard... I love you, Dotty."

"I love you too, Papa," Dotty says, as she pulls out her mother's flowered hanky from her pocket and dabs the moisture in her eyes.

"All aboard!" the uniformed conductor shouts, standing at the entry of the passenger car, looking at his pocket watch.

"Here, Dotty," her father says, handing her the carpet bag and a basket of food. "Your mother packed you some good things to eat along the way."

Dotty nods, and reaches into her purse to find her ticket to Chicago, then hands it to the waiting conductor. He examines the ticket and punches several holes in it. "Right this way, miss," holding her hand while she steps up on the little metal stool and up the steps to the train. Dotty waves one more good-bye to her papa before the conductor closes the train door.

She makes her way down the aisle and chooses a window seat towards the middle. There are plenty of seats to choose from since New Orleans is the beginning of the line and Chicago will be the end. The trip takes over nineteen hours to travel the nine hundred miles to Chicago. *Might as well settle in,* she thinks to herself, as she slings her carpet-bag suitcase onto the overhead rack and gets cozy, Dotty sets the basket of food her mother packed, on the floor.

The train starts to move, making a screeching noise as the gears slowly push the wheels over the metal rails. Picking up speed as it leaves the station, the air around the engine fills with black dense smoke. Dotty leans back into the red leather seat and gazes out the window. Her thoughts start to wander over the past ten years since her mother saw the ghost coming towards her out of the woods. *I am so glad to be out of those creepy old woods and heading for civilization of the big city. Lord, I hated going out at night just to use the shithouse to relieve myself. I rather hold my pee and poo until morning. Wouldn't want to run into that old ghost who haunts our woods. And if that isn't enough, all those spooky sounds at night give me the creeps every time I go out there.*

Dotty's thoughts now turn to Chicago. *My Auntie Ella and Uncle Felix have a lovely upstairs apartment over a bakery shop. The aromas of fresh baked breads and cakes smell heavenly. And they have electric lights and a bathroom inside their apartment. They have a real flush toilet and a porcelain tub. How heavenly to bathe in warm water inside. And just think, no smelly outhouse with spiders hanging off the walls and big black bugs crawling around the floor. And no more Sears Catalog pages to wipe with. Heavenly.*

Dotty dozes off, rocked to sleep by the gentle sway of the passenger train. She dreams of the big city lights; department stores full of clothes and bakeries with delicious chocolate cakes and cream-filled pastries. The train comes to a stop in Jackson, Mississippi and Dotty awakes to more passengers getting on. As they take up the rest of the window seats, Dotty feels the hunger pains in her stomach. *Hm, it must be dinner time. Let's see what Mama packed, two pieces of fried chicken wrapped in paper, a jelly jar of cooked greens and okra, a mason jar of fresh milk, homemade buttermilk biscuits and slice of Mama's German chocolate cake with coconut-pecan icing. Yummy!*

Dotty dives into the chicken leg first, then takes a bite of the fluffy biscuits, wiping her mouth with the cloth napkin her mother included in the basket. She digs around in the basket until she finds a small silver fork her mother packed in the basket to eat her greens and okra. She decides to save the chicken breast and other biscuit for later but cannot resist the cake. Eating it slowly, she savors the chocolate and coconut melting in her mouth and feels like a queen at a banquet. Washing down the whole meal with the fresh milk, she thinks, *This is the best day of my whole life.*

Looking out the window, Dotty sees the sun setting, casting colors of pink and purple on the low hanging clouds. Soon the sky will be dark. The train continues chugging through Mississippi and in a few hours, pulls into Memphis, Tennessee. In the twenty-minute stop, more people board the train.

This time a skinny old black man with a white cane comes tapping down the aisle. He smells of Old Spice cologne. His face is as wrinkled as a dried-up old prune. He is dressed in a well-worn black suit with a white long-sleeved shirt, unbuttoned at the collar. His lace-up leather shoes are thin in the sole and his socks sag around his bony ankles. He wears dark glasses, even though it is dark outside. He taps the vacant seat next to Dotty and asks, "Uh, excuse me, is this here seat taken?"

Dotty looks up at the old blind man and feels the conflict inside her, then answers, "No sir... Take a seat."

"Is it all right by you if I seat here, missy?"

If Dotty were in Alabama, no black man would ask to sit by her. Black folks just wouldn't ask such a question. But this is now Tennessee, and besides, the old man is blind. He cannot tell if Dotty is black or white, young or old. Dotty thinks, *What's the harm.* "No problem, mister. Sit yourself down here. Make yourself comfy. Where you headed?" Dotty asks.

"Thank ya, missy," the old man says, as he shuffles into the vacant seat. "I'm goin' to Effingham, Illinois. I got family up there, a daughter and two grandbabies."

The two chit-chat a little more, then the old man says, "I'm gonna try to snooze a little. Effingham is five o'clock in the mornin'. Don't wanna miss it. Good night, missy."

"Good night, sir," Dotty says, then nods off to sleep herself.

Chapter 9

When Dotty awakes in the morning, the old blind man sitting next to her is gone. She stretches the stiffness out of her body, raising her arms high above her head, arching her back. Daylight shines through the window as the train passes through the countryside.

When the train conductor walks through the passenger car, Dotty reaches out and touches his sleeve asking, "Sir, what time is it and how much longer until Chicago?"

The conductor pulls out his pocket watch and says, "Well, little miss, by my watch, it is eight-fifteen. We have about forty-five minutes until we reach Chicago."

After the conductor leaves, Dotty digs into the lunch and retrieves the last piece of fried chicken and biscuits she saved from yesterday. Hungry from the long train ride, she demolishes the leftovers and washes it down with the rest of her milk. She wipes the milk mustache and crumbs from her face with the napkin in her basket. One more trip to the restroom before Chicago, she thinks to herself. *Now, where is the restroom?*

Seeing a sign above a door at the end of the passenger car, she gets up from her seat and walks toward the sign, swaying back and forth with the gyrations of the train. Inside there are three toilet stalls, two sinks and a huge mirror on the wall. After using the toilet, she washes her hands and face, then fixes her hair. She stares into the mirror, summoning up her courage to start a new life in Chicago and says to herself, *Well, here goes.*

The conductor walks through the train announcing, "Chicago Union Station coming up in ten minutes. Chicago, end of the line."

Dotty hurries back to her seat and reaches up to the overhead rack and grabs her bag with all her worldly possessions. Then looking around her seat, she gathers up her lunch basket; its only contents are the cloth napkin, the silver fork and two glass jars.

As the train pulls into the station, it slows to a jerky stop. Dotty, along with all the other passengers, stands and starts to file down the aisles. Slowly the procession of travelers moves to the end of the passenger car and down the steps to the terminal below. Dotty moves along with the rest of the crowd toward the waiting area of Union Station, holding tightly to her luggage. Soon the long corridor opens into a grand room with over-sized red velvet chairs, grand floor to ceiling murals advertising Cocoa-Cola, the Blackstone Hotel, the Igler Casino, and other businesses in Chicago.

Dotty anxiously looks around for someone who looks like her mother, Margaret, only taller. A woman with dark brown wavy hair and red lipstick stands out in the crowded waiting room of Union Station. She is wearing a red satiny sleeveless dress that falls to her mid-calf, her black high heel shoes clicking on the tile floor, her bare shoulders covered with a silver fox fur. She waves her hands in the air and shouts out, "Dotty! Oh Dotty! Here we are."

The man next to her is very thin. His black hair is slicked back with a pencil thin mustache below his large pointy nose. He has on a pale brown suit with a bowtie, his brown shoes polished to a high shine.

Dotty runs to the couple through the crowd, shouting back, "Auntie Ella, Uncle Felix, is that you?"

"Yes, dear, of course it is. How was your trip? Any problems? Here, give me your bag," says Ella, then turning to Felix says, "Here, Felix, would you please carry Dotty's bag? It's rather heavy."

Felix takes the bag and Ella continues to talk. "How is your dear mother? How is she holding up in that southern wilderness? How many children does she have now, the poor thing? Anne is still at home. She will be excited to see you again. We think we have the perfect job for you. I'll tell you all about it when we get home."

They walk briskly to Felix's 1930 black Ford sedan. Dotty climbs in the back and Ella sits up front with her husband. The waxed exterior shines like a new silver dime. The smooth green leather seats are spotless. Felix takes excessive care of his prize possession since he paid a great deal of money for it. By profession, Felix is a well-paid lithographer and likes to spend his money on luxuries.

The automobile starts up with the turn of a key and push of the gears. They drive a little way to the other side of town where there are lots of shops with apartments on the second floor. Turning down a narrow alley, behind a bakery, Felix pulls into a garage and they all get out. One by one, they walk up the stairs to the second floor and open the door to the kitchen.

Dotty looks around to see a cheerful yellow kitchen with a modern gas stove and porcelain sink. The floral curtains hang in the open windows letting the sunshine in. Grey rolled linoleum covers the kitchen floor under a round wooden table covered in a red and white cotton cloth, with four matching chairs surrounding it. Little plants in pots sit on the windowsills, growing in the sunlight.

"Anne! Anne! We're home. Come out and say hi to your cousin, Dotty," Ella shouts, filling the kettle on the stove with water and lighting the burner under it. "Dotty, how about a cup of tea?"

"Oh… yes, Auntie. Uh, I'd like that." She struggles to find the words. She is tired and numb from the long train ride.

"Dotty! You're finally here," Anne says, bursting into the kitchen with excitement. "Wow, Dotty, you look all grown up now." She notes that Dotty is shapelier than her last visit. Anne, being five years younger than Dotty and an only child, looks up to Dotty like her big sister. They live totally different lives and always have lots to talk about.

Dotty's eyes light up when she sees Anne and she flashes a toothy grin. "Anne, I get to stay here in Chicago. Oh Anne, I'm so happy I don't have to go back to the farm. All the farmers there are so ugly and old. One of the ones we play cards with wanted to marry me. He's so skinny and has a scraggly beard and mustache to hide his missing teeth. Can you imagine? But Mama wouldn't let Papa marry me off to him. No matter how much land he had, he was too old and smelly." The two girls giggle at the thought of it.

"Dotty, come put your stuff in my room, and make yourself at home," Anne says, taking Dotty's hand and leading her through the living room to her bedroom. Dotty glances at the opulence of the sofa and chairs covered with velvet, cut in ornate patterns of flowers and leaves. The heavy drapes covering lace curtains over the windows let little light in, but the beaded Tiffany lamps illuminate the room. The plush dark red and gold carpet muffles the sound of her footsteps. The room smells of tobacco from the crystal ash tray on the shiny varnished end table next to one of the over-stuffed chairs.

As the girls enter Anne's room, Dotty feels a little envious of her cousin, seeing the airy lightness of her bedroom. The lacy ivory curtains match the fluffy ivory eyelet bedspread on Anne's big double bed. A pile of pale pink pillows tops her bed with a large china doll in a pink silk dress amongst all the pillows. Her dresser and mirror are painted white with gold trim. In one corner of the room sits a large two-story dollhouse that is open in the back, so you can see miniature furniture and a tiny family of dolls.

Dotty puts down her bag, then the two girls start jumping on the bed. When they hear Ella shout out, "Stop jumping on the bed!" they stop and whisper secrets to each other and then start giggling and laughing, until their sides hurt.

Chapter 10

The next day, over a breakfast of bacon, eggs, toast and coffee, Ella tells Dotty of a position with a rich Jewish family. Anne starts nibbling on her bacon and Dotty splatters a little ketchup on her scrambled eggs. Felix is already off to work, so Ella sits down with the girls.

She takes a sip of her coffee and then starts to tell Dotty the details of the job opening. "Dotty, I know of a Jewish family in Evanston that needs a nanny to help with their two adopted children. The boy, Johnny, is four years old and the girl, Clara, is two. I am aware of all the help you have given your mother, Margaret, with her five children. I think you can do very well in that position. What do you think, Dotty? Shall I phone up Mrs. Klein for an appointment?"

"Well, Auntie Ella, I have helped my mother for the past eight to ten years with my sisters and brothers, so I reckon I can do it. Only two children, hey?"

"Yes, only two." Ella chuckles a bit. "Frieda Klein and her husband, Bernard, have their hands full with the two little ones. Frieda, who is in her thirties, was once a schoolteacher and has her own way of doing things. She now is very involved in social affairs and needs help with the day-to-day routines of the children.

"Bernard, who is in his fifties, works at one of the big banks in Chicago, so when he comes home at night, he likes things in order. They employ a housekeeper, a cook and a gardener. You will just be responsible for the children."

Dotty listens intently while eating her breakfast at the kitchen table. She has no idea where Evanston is, or who those Jewish people are, but she trusts her auntie. She feels anything is better than being married off to an old bachelor farmer who lives out in the woods. She loves Chicago where her aunt and uncle live and all the conveniences of the big city. "Sounds great, Auntie Ella," Dotty says, finishing off her toast and coffee.

"Good! Then I will ring up Freida and tell her you can work for her," Ella says. She stands up to clear the table of dishes and then walks over to the phone on the wall.

The next morning after breakfast, Ella takes Dotty to Evanston on the CTA, 'L' as they call the elevated train. From the train station, they walk to Dempster Street on the East Side, through the downtown shopping area. They come to a magnificent two-story Tudor mansion, covered with ivy, on a tree lined street.

Dotty can hardly believe her eyes, as she and her aunt walk through the manicured garden to the heavy oak door inlaid with beveled glass and leaded glass windows. To Dotty, it is like walking into a fairy tale castle.

Ella rings the doorbell and after the chimes subside, the housekeeper, a plump older woman in a white dress and apron, opens the door and says, "Can I help you?"

"Yes. I am Mrs. Ella Cohen. I have an appointment with Mrs. Frieda Klein. I've brought my niece, Dotty, who is interested in the position of nanny," Ella tells the housekeeper standing in the doorway in her white sensible saddle shoes. Her stern look melts into a smile.

"Oh, Mrs. Klein is waiting for you in the library," she says, eying fourteen-year-old Dotty. The housekeeper leads Dotty and her Aunt Ella to the library. Dark wood bookcases line the walls. Books of every size and color fill the cases from ceiling to floor. Never has Dotty seen so many books outside the public library in Mobile. She soaks up the atmosphere, her eyes thirsty to read all that she sees.

Mrs. Klein motions for Dotty and her aunt to sit in two ornate upholstered chairs across from where she sits in a wooden swivel chair behind a huge oak desk. Mrs. Klein begins talking about the position to Ella, while Dotty gazes around the massive room in a daze.

"Now, Mrs. Cohen, Dotty's primary purpose in this position will be to care for the children. As you can see, my husband and I are getting on in years. We cannot have children, so we adopted the two siblings from the Cradle Orphanage. We have a room for Dotty close to the children's room. She will get up with them, dress them, feed them, then take them for a walk in the park after breakfast. Then returning home, the children will go down for their naps. Upon waking, the children will lunch with me then play in their rooms until dinnertime. Dotty will bathe them afterwards, then put them to bed. She will also be responsible for daily tidying up the children's room. She will have Saturday night and all-day Sunday off. She will also have one week vacation a year in the summer. Oh, and we will provide Dotty with a uniform for her to wear while working here. Any questions?"

By now, Dotty has just one question. She tugs on her Aunt Ella's sleeve and whispers in her ear, "Uh, Aunt Ella, how much will she pay me?"

Ella speaks up and asks, "Yes, Mrs. Klein, what does the position pay?"

"The position pays ten dollars a week plus room and board. Do we have a deal?" asks Mrs. Klein.

Dotty nods to her aunt.

Ella smiles and says, "Yes, indeed. When do you wish Dotty to start?"

"Next Monday morning at eight will be fine." Mrs. Klein smiles back.

For the next ten years, Dotty works for Mrs. Klein as the nanny in the great house in Chicago. Once a year she takes the train back home to Alabama to help her mother with spring cleaning. Fearing an encounter with the ghost who haunts the woods around the farmhouse, Dotty takes care to be inside when the sun goes down.

In the next few years, her sisters move to Chicago and Aunt Ella finds jobs for the girls. Then every

Saturday night, the sisters dress up and take the 'L' to Chicago. They shop for clothes and go dancing at the Aragon Ballroom to the tunes of the big bands playing there.

Chapter 11

The Aragon Ballroom, completed in 1926, is designed in the Moorish architectural style. With its extraordinary design and aesthetics, the Aragon Ballroom becomes one of Chicago's premier live entertainment venues. At a cost of two million dollars, it is one of the most elaborate places of its time. Soon after its opening, the Aragon Ballroom is called 'the most beautiful ballroom in the world.' Crystal chandeliers, mosaic tiles, beautiful arches, extravagant balconies and terracotta ceilings combine to create a truly magnificent and unique site. Even the ceiling looks like the sky when clouds move across the stars. The interior resembles, in various ways, a Spanish village and is named for a region of Spain. The Aragon is an immediate success and remains a popular Chicago attraction throughout the 1940s.

According to legend, secret tunnels under the nearby Green Mill bar, a Prohibition-era hangout of Al Capone, lead to the Aragon's basement.

Its proximity to the Chicago 'L' provides patrons with easy access. Often crowds as many as eighteen thousand attend during each six-day business week.

The ballroom hosts nearly all the top big bands that young single people come to dance and listen to, in hopes of meeting someone special.

It is there at the Aragon Ballroom that Dotty meets Al, a tall Jewish Hungarian immigrant with thick black hair, dressed in a pin-striped double-breasted suit. The band is playing a rumba and Al asks Dotty to dance.

"Oh no, I don't know how to dance the rumba," Dotty says, blushing as she looks up into his warm brown eyes.

"Come on. I'll teach you," Al insists, taking her by the hand and leading Dotty onto the dance floor. Al puts one hand on Dotty's upper shoulder and starts moving his feet and hips. Then he places his other hand around her slender waist.

"Just follow my lead. It goes step, swish, swish, step. Got it?" says Al, moving Dotty around the dance floor. Then he turns her unexpectedly, and Dotty steps on Al's toes.

"Oh! I'm so sorry."

"No problem. You're doing just fine. Don't worry. Just feel the music in your sway," Al says, smiling at Dotty's attempts to follow his lead.

The music stops and they walk off the dance floor together and start talking to each other. Al doesn't want to let this petite lovely lady go. At twenty-five, Dotty is stunning, dressed to the nines in a clingy black dress and black high heeled pumps. Her reddish-brown hair is permed in the latest style, her blue eyes framed in thick lashes and her lips, a luscious ruby red.

Dotty's sister, Helen, and cousins, Anne and Mitzi, stare at the two from afar with mouths wide open. They can't believe little Dotty caught the handsomest man in the ballroom.

"Look at those two. Dotty doesn't even dance well," says Helen, revealing her jealousy.

"Yeah. I can dance better than Dotty, and I'm a cripple," says Mitzi, who wears a six-inch block on her left shoe. Childhood polio has left her with one leg shorter than the other.

"Well, good for her. It's about time. Dotty deserves a nice guy." Anne smiles at the hope of a budding romance for her cousin. Anne remembers when Dotty first arrived in Chicago from Alabama, so awkward and so thin. She now sees the elegant transformation of Dotty. Dotty even smokes cigarettes because everyone in high society is doing it.

"Just look at her! She's charmed that fine-looking man on the dance floor, and she can't even dance. Let's go, girls," her sister, Helen says, ready to leave.

"Wait, Helen, we can't leave yet. They're playing a slow dance. Smile, girls," Anne says.

"Hey, that big good-looking guy and his two tall friends are coming our way. Maybe they will ask one of us to dance," Mitzi says, making sure her long sapphire blue gown conceals her specialized shoe.

And sure enough, all three girls are asked to dance to the music. They dance the foxtrot and the waltz. They dance until their toes hurt in their high heeled shoes. They dance all evening on that warm and starry night.

Chapter 12

As weeks turn into months, Dotty's love for Al grows. One cold December day, Al drops to one knee and asks Dotty to marry him. He pulls out a little black box from his shirt pocket and opens it for Dotty to see. Sparkling in the box is a diamond ring set in a gold band.

Dotty's eyes widen and her mouth drops open. She is overwhelmed and struggles to say, "Yes, Al... I will marry you!"

That evening, alone in her room, she writes to her parents in Alabama to tell them the good news. Her mother, Margaret, writes back.

She and her father cannot travel to Chicago in the dead of winter for a wedding. She is pregnant again.

Al's mother has moved to California for her health and cannot travel to Chicago either. Disappointed by the prospect of neither of their parents' ability to come for a wedding, Al and Dotty decide they might as well get married at City Hall.

Dotty calls her Aunt Suzie who lives in Chicago to tell her the good news.

"Oh, Dotty, I'm so happy for you! When? Where? Is your mother coming?" Aunt Suzie asks excitedly, her words flying out like a flock of geese heading south.

"Mama and Papa can't come because Mama's pregnant again," Dotty explains.

"Pregnant again! At forty-five years old? What is that woman thinking?" Suzie fumes.

"Well, you know Daddy. The more children the more help with the farming," Dotty says, defending her mother. She is grateful her mother sent her to Chicago. Grateful she did not stay in Alabama to marry a farmer and end up barefoot and pregnant every two years.

"Well, tell me about your young man and how did you meet him. When do you plan to marry?"

"Oh, Aunt Suzie, He's so dreamy. He's tall and handsome like Clark Gable. He has jet black hair and deep brown eyes. I just melt when he looks at me," Dotty gushes. "I met him dancing at the Aragon Ballroom, with Anne, Mitzi and Helen. He knows all the latest dances and leads me around the dance floor like a dream. His name is Alex and he's from Hungary or maybe it's Rumania, anyways, Eastern Europe. You would like him, Aunt Suzie, he's such a gentleman. He's not grabby or vulgar like most of the men I've met, who only want one thing. He doesn't have a car, which is good. Lots of men offer to drive you home, then they put the moves on you when they have you in their car. It's kind of scary. But Al takes me home on the 'L' and doesn't try any monkey business, just kisses me good night."

"How old is he, Dotty?"

"He is just a few years older than me, around twenty-eight years old."

"And when do you and Alex plan to tie the knot?"

"Next Saturday at City Hall. Since neither of our parents can come, we'll just have a civil wedding. Then maybe we will go out to dinner afterwards."

"Well, Dotty, you and Alex must come to dinner at my house after you two marry. I will make you a nice dinner to celebrate."

"Thank you for the invitation, Auntie. That will be great. See you next Saturday, as a 'married' woman! It's a date," Dotty says and hangs up the phone.

***

Al's letter to his Jewish mother, Ethel, in California is received with anger and frustration. This Dotty her son wants to marry is not Jewish. Ethel is not happy about this situation. So, she calls her sister, Rina, in Chicago to complain.

"How dare that little Protestant tart marry my son, Alex! Why can't Al marry a nice Jewish girl and have children raised properly, in the Jewish traditions?" Ethel protests.

"I didn't know Al was engaged and there are certainly plenty of Jewish ladies in Chicago."

"I know, I know, Rina. But what can I do to stop it?" Ethel pleads.

"Well Ethel, what do you know about this girl Alex is about to marry?" Rina questions.

"Only that her name is Dotty Pimperl. She works for Frieda and Barnard Klein as a nanny for their two adopted children in Evanston," Ethel answers through clenched teeth.

"I know Frieda Klein from the Jewish Women's Society. She lives on Dempster Street. Her husband's a banker. Ethel, I'll go and talk to the girl and maybe I can discourage her from marrying Alex," Rina tells her sister, even though her heart aches for the young woman named Dotty. Who is she to break up a romance? At least she can warn the poor girl of her future mother-in-law.

"Thanks, Rina, I owe you. By the way, if you ever get tired of the cold weather and snow in Chicago, come to Los Angeles. The sun is always shining, and the weather is always warm."

"I'll think about it, Ethel. Good talking to you. Bye for now," Rina closes.

"Goodbye, Rina. May God be with you," Ethel says and hangs up the phone.

The next day, Rina shows up at the house where Dotty works and knocks on the front door. The housekeeper comes to the door and asks, "Can I help you?"

"Yes, does a Dotty Pimperl live or work here?" Rina asks, feeling awkward.

"Why, yes. Who may I say is calling?" the housekeeper asks, wondering why anyone would be asking for the nanny.

My name is Rina, her finance's aunt.

"Oh." Answers the housekeeper, then turns and leaves the room.

A few minutes later, Dotty comes to the door.

"Hi. Are you Dotty?"

"Why yes. Who are you?"

"I'm Rina."

"Rina? Do I know you?" Dotty asks wondering why anyone would seek her out.

"Miss Pimperl, I am Alex's Aunt Rina, his mother's sister. I've come to warn you about Al's mother in California. She is very protective of her youngest son and does not approve of mixed religious marriages. Al is Jewish and she does not approve of you, a Protestant, marrying her son. She can make life miserable for you and Al," Rina says, shaking her head.

"But she's in California and we're here in Chicago. What can she possibly do to us?" Dotty's nervousness comes out in her high-pitched voice.

"Even though she is my little sister, I know how manipulative and divisive she can be. I'm just warning you, don't marry Alex. But if you do, for your sake, do not move to California," Rina says with dread in her tone of voice.

The next Saturday, Dotty marries Al at the Chicago City Hall, regardless of Rina's warning. She and Alex stop by her Aunt Suzie's home for dinner as promised. To their surprise, the whole house is full of friends and cousins, aunts and uncles offering congratulations. Everyone brings a scrumptious dish. Wine and beer flow freely, and a huge white cake with red roses and lettering saying, '*Congratulations Alex and Dotty*' sits on the lace covered table, ready to be cut.

Chapter 13

War breaks out in Europe shortly after Dotty's first child is born. She and Al are happily living in one of the three story brownstone flats near the North Side of Chicago. However, the Draft Board in Illinois is drafting men for Hitler's war in Europe.

On the morning of Dotty and Al's first anniversary, a letter arrives from Al's mother. Dotty hangs over Al's shoulder as he opens the envelope and unfolds the letter. He reads:

Al, I am worried you will be sucked into the terrible war in Europe. Many of my Jewish relatives and friends who remained in Satu Mare are gone. If they are not killed by Nazis, they are taken to labor camps to work until they drop, then burnt up in ovens.

Come to California. It is the last state to draft for the horrible war in Europe. You and your little family, Dotty, and the baby, will be safe here. Come to Los Angeles where I live. It is nice and warm here. Not so cold as Chicago. The air, it is so wonderfully fresh, and the Pacific Ocean is close by. Come to California. You can live with me until you are settled. You will never want to go back.

Love, Mother

Al turns to Dotty; his eyes widen, searching for the answer to his mother's letter. "Well, Dotty, what do you think? Should we risk moving to California or risk me being drafted and shipped to fight in Europe and possibly get shot? You know, Dotty, I've never shot a gun before. Not like your brothers who grew up in the Alabama woods. Tell me, what do you think we should do?"

Dotty's heart sinks thinking of leaving all her friends and family in Chicago. She thinks about what Al's Aunt Rina said about her Jewish mother-in-law, who wanted her youngest son to marry a nice Jewish girl. She worries she will be alone in California in strange, unfamiliar surroundings with just Al and her little baby boy she is still breast feeding. But her fear of Al being drafted and sent to Europe to be killed in some senseless war, is more than her fear of moving to California.

Summoning up her courage, Dotty manages to smile back at Al and say, "Well, if your mother thinks it best, maybe we should move to California. If you go first and get settled, I can take the train down to Alabama and stay with my mother and father on the farm. But only until you find a nice apartment for the three of us."

Dotty dreams of the mild weather in southern Alabama and the smell of pine trees around the old farmhouse. She has not seen her parents or brothers for a while. She yearns for the yummy taste of her mother's cooking and the feel of her father's warm embrace. She longs to hear her brother's jokes and funny stories of what's been happening since she left home.

So, Dotty and Al make plans to leave Chicago. They each write to their parents of their intent to move from Chicago and relocate in Los Angeles. Then they give away or sell the things they don't need and pack up the rest. Dotty opens her big black trunk she uses for a coffee table that sits in front of their sofa. She carefully folds and packs her clothes and the baby things in the old trunk along with a few treasured items. Then she washes and folds Al's clothes and packs them in their one battered suitcase for his trip to the west coast.

Soon they are ready to go. Dotty and Al make love one more time before taking a cab to the train station. It will be a long time before they see each other again. Al takes the train headed west to California and Dotty, with baby in tow, boards the train traveling south to Alabama.

Chapter 14

After five days on the train, Al arrives in Los Angeles Union Station in the heart of downtown. His mother anxiously paces the marble inlaid floor of the spacious waiting room. It has been several years since Ethel moved to California. She has missed her son who stayed in Chicago to marry the Protestant girl, Dotty Pimperl. She has never met Dotty who now has a son by Alex, her first grandson. *Oh, how I wish Alex would have married a nice Jewish girl...* she thinks to herself... *but he didn't. What's done is done. Might as well make the best of it.*

Alex walks through the double doors into the Art Deco waiting room and Ethel greets him with a big smile and a warm hug. "Alex, so good to see you, my son! Are you hungry? There's a good deli here in the train station. They have delicious pastrami sandwiches on rye. All kosher."

"Thanks, Mother, but I'm not that hungry. Had a bite on the train. Just really tired from the long trip," Al says, putting down his heavy suitcase packed full of all his clothes.

"Then we will just take a cab to my flat. It's not very far from here. We can grab a taxi out in front of the station," his mother says.

74

Alex picks up his suitcase and follows his mother through the waiting room out to the street in front. Choosing the first cab in the line, the driver opens their door for them.

"Twelve-twenty-one Burlingame Street, please," Ethel says to the driver. Then turning to Alex, she says, "I have bad news," Ethel pauses to take a deep breath. "The Japanese bombed Pearl Harbor in Hawaii, surprise attacks, the morning of December 7th." She takes another deep breath to steady herself. "Their planes hit all eight of our Navy's battleships, destroying four of them and damaging the rest… Also, three cruisers, three destroyers, a hundred eighty-eight aircraft are damaged or sank, and killed over two thousand Americans."

"Oh my God, Mother. I thought we left all that madness in Europe," Alex shouts out angrily, shaking his head in disbelief.

"Al… the worst part…" his mother pauses again, feeling her heart pounding in her chest.

"What is it, Mother?" Al asks, seeing his mother squeezing back the tears in her eyes.

"The Army… is now drafting here in California for the war in the Pacific Islands. Hawaii, Guam, the Philippines and other islands, the Japanese want them all, like Hitler and Mussolini want all of Europe. There's no stopping them."

"Oh my God…" Alex says, looking down at the wedding ring on his left hand. He thinks about Dotty and his new baby boy. How he hated to leave Dotty and the baby in Alabama. What a nightmare. What now? What if he is drafted? What if he is sent to the Pacific Ocean to fight a war, he knows nothing of? What if he gets shot and dies, leaving Dotty a widow to raise their infant son?

The taxicab comes to a large stucco duplex and parks next to the curb. "Here we are, twelve-twenty-one Burlingame Street. That will be four dollars and fifty cents."

"I got it, Mother." Alex says, pulling a five-dollar bill out of his wallet, hands it to the driver and says, "Keep the change."

"Thanks," the driver says, opening the car door, then opening the trunk to pull out Al's suitcase. "Here you go. Welcome to California!"

Chapter 15

At the train station in Bay Minette, Alabama, Dotty waits on the platform next to the tracks in the early morning. She holds her six-month baby boy on one hip, grasping a small suitcase with her other hand, while her large black trunk rests at her feet. Her papa is late, as usual. She looks up at the towering pines and magnolias and smells the crisp morning air. She sees a bright red cardinal resting on a limb, in one of the many crimson azalea bushes. The bird is building a nest of twigs for its mate. It is spring in southern Alabama, the air is so sweet, Dotty can taste it. It is a far cry from the cold, smoky dampness of Chicago.

HONK! HONK! HONK! Dotty looks up the road and sees a black Ford farm truck, with her papa behind the wheel. Clouds of smoke and dust bellow up behind the fat rear tires. The truck pulls up to the train platform and Dotty's papa jumps out.

"Hey, Dotty! What ya got there on your hip? That my first grandson? My Lord! Look at that chubby lil' fella," he says, gently pinching the baby's chubby dimpled cheeks with his calloused fingers. "And all that curly red hair on that sweet lil' ol' baby! You can sure tell he's a Pimperl."

"It's good to be home, Papa," Dotty says, putting down her suitcase to hug her father, and kisses him on the cheek. She feels a warm glow as her lips brush her father's freshly shaven face.

"Oh, it's so good to see you, Dotty. You're as beautiful as ever, and that lil' boy of your'n, what a handful! Here, let me hold him," her father says, as Dotty shifts her baby from her hip to her papa's strong arms. "Oh my, he's as heavy as a sack of potatoes... sweet potatoes!" he says. They both laugh and Dotty's baby smiles and giggles back, showing off his first two teeth.

"Here, Dotty, let's get going," her papa says, handing the blue-eyed baby back to Dotty. "Your mama can hardly wait to see our new grandson. She has fried chicken and okra waiting. Are you hungry?"

"Yes, sir! I am," Dotty says, thinking about the taste of her mama's crispy fried chicken and homegrown okra. Her mouth waters for her favorite southern foods.

Her father loads the heavy black trunk into the flat bed, tying it to the slats with heavy rope to keep it from sliding around. Then helping Dotty and the baby into the cab of the truck, he lifts the small suitcase in after her.

Dotty's thoughts of home swirl around in her head. She thinks about how the small country town has changed. Small businesses dot the area around the train station and gas stations are on nearly every corner, combined with groceries and sundries, as well as a counter to sit at for cold drinks and beer. They head down highway thirty-one toward the farm and she looks at the pine trees, lining the highway on either side, as far as the eye can see.

Her thoughts turn to the old man who was murdered in the woods and the ghost her mother saw that night coming out of the forest toward her. Her pregnant mother so frightened, she fainted and hit her head on a rock. She remembers how scared she was; being the oldest of four girls, the responsibility of the house would fall on her shoulders if her mother died. Since that night, Dotty has been afraid to be out in the woods after dark. She does not want to run into any haunting spirits in the woods. And what about the murderers who killed old man Gelsinger and burnt down his shack?

The bumpy ride in the truck rocks her baby boy to sleep as they travel down the road, and it's the perfect time to ask.

"Papa…"

"Yes, Dotty?"

"Do you remember the night when Mama saw the ghost?"

"Yes, Dotty. How can I forget?"

"Well, did they ever find the men who murdered old man Gelsinger?"

"Yes, indeed. The sheriff found them, all right. One was a worker that Ralph Slade hired to pick cotton that year. The other was thought to be a drifter from

Tennessee. They each got seven years in the prison out in Atmore. Mama goes out there and preaches the gospel to the inmates there. Turns out one of them found Jesus. Turned his life around. When he got out, I gave him a job tapping turpentine in our piney woods. A good worker, he was. He saved up his wages and headed for the Texas oilfields. The other one, the drifter, got into trouble with the law again and is back in jail. Some never learn."

"Papa... what about all the money Gelsinger hid? Did anyone ever find it?"

"Nope. Ya' know, the house was burnt down to the ground. Some folks took to looking around in the ash, but no one's found anything yet. The forest pretty much swallowed the whole thing up by now. Hard to see where his ol' shack once was. He has no kin that we know of, so I guess ol' Mother Earth claims his buried treasure."

They turn off highway thirty-one onto route two, the dirt road that leads to the old farmhouse. Soon Dotty sees her mother run out the door to greet her and the first grandchild.

Margaret is overwhelmed by the sight of Dotty and her baby. Tears of joy and emotion flood Margaret's eyes. She embraces her daughter and child and feels her heart bursting with happiness. *Thank you, God. My Dotty is home,* is her silent prayer.

Chapter 16

Ever since Al boarded the train to California, he misses Dotty and his baby boy. His heart aches more each day they are apart. He remembers their last day together in Chicago, in each other's embrace, her soft white skin, her deep blue eyes. He remembers their passion together, one last time. Every evening, he sits on his bed in the barracks writing his beloved wife to calm the ache in his heart.

***

Every afternoon, Dotty puts her precious baby down for a nap. While the infant sleeps, Dotty walks to Demco's store, down the dirt road and across the highway.

"Any mail for me, Shirley?" she asks the young girl behind the counter.

"Yes, ma'am! Another letter from California. Here you go," she replies.

Dotty's heart leaps. Another letter from Al. She waits until she runs back to the farmhouse to open the letter. Sitting on the wooden porch swing, she opens the letter and reads out loud:

My Darling Dotty,

I miss you so much. Life under my mother's roof is a living hell. Worse yet, I am drafted. They sent me to Camp Pendleton. They shaved all my hair off. I sleep in barracks with 39 other guys. They wake us up at 5 in the morning and they march us around the compound. Then they take us out in field to shoot guns and test us. Dotty, I cannot hit that target to save my life. I do not want to kill anyone. I fail the shooting tests. Not like other men. So, they make me a cook. This is worst job I ever have.

I miss you, Dotty, and the life in Chicago. I miss you, Dotty. Come to California. Stay with my mother until I get out of this damn army. You and the baby get on a train and come out west. My heart is breaking without you. I cannot wait to see you again.

All my love,
Al

Dotty puts down the letter after reading it. She feels her stomach churning again. She jumps off the swing, leans over the porch and vomits in the grass. Her breasts ache. She is pregnant again. That last goodbye before leaving Chicago did it. She hasn't told anyone yet. *I won't be able to keep my little secret for too long*, she thinks, feeling panicky. *Better make those train reservations soon, while the baby can travel free,* she contemplates.

Her mother, Margaret, is in the kitchen, baking bread for the day. The smell of yeast fills the warm room when Dotty walks in. Margaret continues to push and pull the dough with her hands into a smooth round ball, slapping it from time to time on the wooden counter.

Looking up from her work, Margaret says, "Oh... hi, Dotty."

"Mama... uh... I got another letter from Al."

"Oh? What did he have to say?" Margaret asks.

"Well, Mama... He wants me to come to California..." Dotty answers, the bitter words sticking in her throat.

"Oh... When?" Margaret asks, pausing from working the bread dough.

"Soon... He sent me money for the train fare," Dotty says, torn between family and husband. She tries to hold back her tears, keeping her fears to herself. Another baby on the way without the help of her own mother. What if Al's mother doesn't like her? What if she doesn't like California? What if... what if... what if...

"Well, Dotty, if Al wants you to join him in California, then you must go," Margaret says, gently touching Dotty's hand. She suspects there is something else Dotty is not telling her but decides not to press her. "I recall when your father wanted to move to Alabama, and I had you and your sister and one on the way. It was a big change for me too. But you'll be fine. You go to your husband in California. I'll tell Papa to order the train tickets for you. You're strong and you'll be fine." Margaret smiles to hide the pain in her heart.

Dotty writes to Al; she tells him, she is coming in a week, but does not tell him she is six months pregnant.

Dotty gets on board the train from Alabama to Los Angeles, California. There, in Los Angeles General Hospital, Stella is born.

PART 2
June 1960

Chapter 17

In 1960, Alabama, along with other southern states, is struggling with civil rights protests. Black people below the Mason-Dixon line are treated like second class citizens. They are forced to sit in the back of trains and buses. They are forced to use separate public schools as well as separate public facilities, such as restrooms and water fountains. Anger is boiling over in the big cities in the southern part of the United States. Men in white sheets, their faces hidden, terrorize the Black communities to keep the colored folks in line.

In 1960, California is a melting pot of many races and religions. Not just Black and White, but Chinese, Korean, Japanese, Mexican, Central and South American families live in California, looking for a better life. Many different Protestant and Catholic churches as well as Jewish synagogues serve the diverse communities.

In 1960, Margaret's granddaughter, living in California, is protesting for her own civil rights. Stella, lanky and awkward at fourteen years old, can't stand the teasing from her older brother and his friends. Her solution is to run away and live with her maternal grandmother in Alabama. She saves all her babysitting money and announces to her mother, "I hate it here! The boys bug me all the time. I want to go live with my grandma in Alabama. I've saved enough money for a one-way ticket on the train to Alabama. I want to leave in June when I get out of school. You can't stop me. I've got my own money," Stella shouts in her high-pitched voice.

Dotty stares at her daughter in disbelief. Never has she heard Stella talk back like that in anger. Her green eyes blaze in defiance, catching her mother totally off guard. *When did my sweet little daughter become so bitchy? Could it be PMS already?* Dotty thinks to herself. *Maybe a break will do her good. Let my mother in Alabama deal with the Drama Queen for the summer.* "Well, Stella," Dotty takes a deep breath, "if you have your mind set... I will write to your grandmother asking if it's okay for you to stay with her for the summer. If she says 'yes' I will ask your dad to buy you a train ticket to Alabama..."

"Oh, Mama! I love you!" Stella's mood changes from confrontation to jubilation. She throws her arms around her mother's neck and hugs her with all her might. Her mother hugs back with a smile thinking it is as much a break for her as it is for her daughter. *Maybe that snotnose brat of mine will learn some manners and respect. Oh well, it's worth a try.*

"Thank you, Mother! Thank you. Thank you. Thank you. You're the best! Now, I must sort through my things and figure out what to pack."

"All right, Stella, when I get the word from your grandmother, I'll let Dad know we will have one less mouth to feed this summer. Now run along, before I change my mind."

Chapter 18

Sunday night at eight o'clock, the sun is setting and all the streetlights glow in the darkening sky. Dotty and Al drive Stella to the train station downtown. It is mid-June and Stella has finished the ninth grade with good marks. As promised, she will spend the summer with her grandmother in Alabama. They wait in the ticket line to buy a seat on the Sunset Limited from Los Angeles to New Orleans. In New Orleans there will be a five-hour layover then a change of trains for another three-hour ride to Bay Minette on the Gulf Breeze. It's a three-day journey, traveling two thousand miles by rail.

While waiting in line, Dotty feels her stomach churning. She wants to tell Stella about the dangers in the thick forests surrounding the old farmhouse. There are too many things that can happen to a young, naïve girl like Stella. Dotty doesn't want to scare her daughter but feels the need to warn her about the Alabama wilderness.

They reach the ticket window and Dotty speaks to the clerk at the counter, while Al and Stella stand silent. "One-way ticket to Bay Minette, Alabama please... Uh, for my daughter, Stella," Dotty says, shaking a little from nervousness. The clerk does her job as she accepts the ninety dollars and prints out the tickets. She hands the tickets over to Dotty, and they turn to walk to the gate.

"Wait… there are somethings I must tell you, Stella," Dotty says, stopping in front of the overstuffed chairs in the Art Deco waiting room. Al puts down Stella's suitcase while Stella still holds on to her green plastic tote.

"What is it, Mama? I don't want to miss my train," Stella says, worried about her mother's long lectures. She is anxious to start her journey.

"Stella, I want you to promise me, you won't go wandering off in the woods by yourself… especially at night," her mother cautions her one and only daughter.

"Why, Mama? I'm not a baby, you know!" Stella scolds her mother.

"Well… snakes. There are lots and lots of snakes out there. You got to look out for snakes," Dotty asserts, covering up her real fear.

"Mama, I'm not afraid of snakes and critters. One of my brother's friends has a snake for a pet and he lets me hold it. They feel funny but not slimy like I thought," Stella says, brushing the thought aside.

"Well… then… I must tell you, dear, the forest around the farmhouse is… haunted," Dotty says slowly, not wanting to scare Stella, just warn her.

"Really, Mama? I'm already fourteen years old. I don't believe in ghosts," Stella says talking back.

"You ask your grandma in Alabama about the ghost she saw in the woods. She'll tell you. It's the truth," Dotty tells her to set the records straight.

"Now, Dotty, don't scare our little girl," Al says, touching her arm.

"Now boarding the Sunset Limited at Gate Seven. All passengers heading for Flagstaff, El Paseo, San Antonio, Biloxi, and final destination New Orleans, please proceed to Gate Seven," the loudspeaker announces.

"That's me! Let's go," Stella shouts, grabbing her suitcase in her free hand.

They walk down the long corridor to Gate Seven, hug, kiss and shed a few tears. Stella steps up into the passenger car. She waves goodbye. The train begins to move, and she is on her way to a different culture. To Alabama, where there once were slaves and now segregation. Where the civil rights movement began in Montgomery when a black woman did not give up her seat to a white man on a bus in 1955. She will see, firsthand, where black people are treated differently than white people, not like the state she grew up in. And Stella will question, "Why?"

Chapter 19

Stella walks through the coach section of the train looking for a seat by the window. There are plenty to choose from since Los Angeles is the beginning of the line. She grabs a window seat and settles in, putting her suitcase in the overhead rack and her tote full of snacks, books, and toiletries on the floor next to her feet. The train fills up with passengers headed east and soon the conductor yells out, "All aboard!"

Tilting her seat back and lifting her feet up on the footrest, Stella relaxes and gazes out the window. As the train pulls out of the train station into the open, her thoughts soar like a canary, released from her cage. She hums a little tune, thinking of the freedom to travel across the United States on her own. The whole country will whiz past her eyes, as if by a magic movie, while she sits by the window. Her eyelids heavy, they slowly close. She hears the distant clatter of the rails rolling over the tracks and the gentle sway of the train lulls her to sleep.

Dreams appear in Stella's subconscious as she wonders what the summer will be like in rural Alabama. The words of her mother, "I must tell you, dear, the forest around the farmhouse is… haunted," echo in her ear. She visualizes the old wooden farmhouse and the forest nearby. How grey the pine trees look next to the vivid green tall grass. The clear blue of the sky seems to darken to purple and points of light pop out from fireflies flitting about.

A shadowy spirit concealed by a pale gauzy covering comes out of the woods, its arms outstretched... reaching... beckoning to Stella in the dream. She wants to run. But she stands her ground to tell the ghostly figure, she is not afraid. She wants to ask, why is it in her dreams. Instead, Stella, in the dream, says to the apparition, "Who are you? And do you have a gift for me?" The ghost says in a whispery voice, "Gelsinger." Then he nods to Stella in the dream and says, "Gold... Silver." Then the ghost fades into the forest and Stella awakes to see the conductor walking through the train.

"Flagstaff coming up," he shouts. "Next stop is Flagstaff, Arizona. If Flagstaff is your destination, gather your baggage and move to the end of the car for departure."

Stella looks at her watch and sees it is almost noon. Her grumbling stomach tells her it is lunchtime. She taps the conductor's arm as he passes and asks, "Excuse me, sir, which way to the dining car?"

"Three cars back," the conductor replies. Then as an afterthought he says, "There's also snacks available below the observation car, the next car back."

A few people get up to walk to the exit for Flagstaff. Stella stands and makes her way to the dining car.

Heavy sliding doors at end of each car, connect the train together. She walks past other passengers sleeping or reading to pass the time. When she reaches the dining car, a uniformed waiter greets her.

"How many in your party for lunch today, miss?"

"Just me," Stella says with a smile.

"Very good, miss. Just follow me," the waiter says, as he leads her to a table with three other diners. Stella sits down and looks at the menu. Everything looks good. She decides to play it safe and orders a hamburger, French fries and a garden salad with ranch dressing.

Lunch arrives on a heavy china plate with silverware wrapped in a linen napkin. "Will there be anything else?" the waiter asks.

"Oh yes, a slice of that apple pie with some vanilla ice cream on the side," Stella says, feeling this is the time to splurge. Everyone at her table agrees to have dessert as well.

The conversations with the others center around where one is going and where one comes from. After eating her lunch, Stella pays for her lunch and then heads for the observation car. When she enters, she can see all around. There are windows on both sides of the car as well as windows on the ceiling. Cozy swivel chairs and benches line either side of the car. In the middle of the car, there are stairs that lead to the snack café below, where you can get anything from hot dogs and sandwiches to chips, pretzels, muffins and coffee or sodas. You can even buy playing cards, to pass the time.

In the back of the café sits a half dozen teenagers around a table. "Come join us," one boy shouts out at Stella. To her delight, Stella joins the group of young travelers. She is happy to have someone to talk to on the long journey to Alabama.

Chapter 20

Stella sits down with the two girls and four boys surrounding the table in the lounge café below the observation car. Janet, who is thirteen and Joanne, fifteen, are sisters. Janet wears her long brown hair in a ponytail, her green eyes peek out from under her bangs. She is a bit chubby from munching on too many potato chips and sodas. She wears a sweatshirt to cover up her pudgy body. As she snacks on salty pretzels, she says nothing.

Joanne is shorter than her sister, but slender with gentle curves. Her bleached blond hair is cut in a short bob, showing off pearl earrings. Joanne accents her puberty with pale pink lipstick and azure blue eyeshadow to flirt with the boys on board. She wears tight blue jeans and a low-cut purple top to show off the beginnings of cleavage. Joanne is the chatty one, wanting to know everything about everyone.

"Hey, girl, what's your name?" Joanne calls out with a nod to Stella.

"I'm Stella. What's yours?" Stella replies, looking over at Joanne and thinking how pretty she is. Stella is still flat as a board, still waiting to fill her bra with something other than tissues. Maybe next year when she is in high school, her mother will let her wear lipstick.

"I'm Joanne and this here is my sister, Janet. We're traveling to Houston to spend the summer with our dad. Our parents divorced two years ago, and we mostly live with our mother in L.A. She's so strict. We can't go anywhere on school nights, and no parties."

"Yeah, no parties," adds Janet, agreeing with her sister. "We can't wait to get to Texas and the freedom we have with our dad. He lets us go to shopping malls on our own and buy things. He even lets us go to some movies, as long as, well, you know they don't have anything... like naked people in them." Janet blushes at the thought of the forbidden.

"Yeah. And the boys in Houston are so cute, with cowboy hats and boots, wearing blue jeans and tee shirts, with muscles busting out from working on farms. They're much cuter than the boys in L.A.," Joanne says, smiling at the comparison, exposing her braces. Running her tongue over her teeth, she says, "I can't wait to get these braces off my teeth, so I can kiss boys," she says with a giggle.

"Oh yeah?" Mark says with a smirk. "You girls sound a little too stuck up for athletes like Ronnie and me." Ronnie and Mark are both seventeen and best friends. Both are tall and thin, wearing jeans and muscles busting out of their tee shirts. Both boys sport crew cuts and are on the high school varsity basketball team.

"Oh yeah? So, you guys are way too tall for me. You look like you could hunt ducks with a rake," Joanne remarks. The others laugh. Now eyeing the buff boys with interest, Joanne asks, "So, where are you guys going?"

"Mark and I are on our way to the Colorado mountains," Ronnie says, running his fingers through his carrot red hair. "We've been planning this backpacking trip in the Colorado mountains since spring. We're meeting up with Mark's cousin, Ray, in Albuquerque. He has a car and the three of us will drive up to Colorado and do some backpacking in the high country."

"Hey, Stella, how about you? Where are you going?" Mark asks, looking at Stella through his hazel-green eyes, his light brown hair spiked up with hair-goo.

"I'm going to Bay Minette, Alabama…"

"With a banjo on your knee?" Ronnie teases.

"No!" Stella shouts back, "I'm going to spend the summer on my grandparents' farm. I get off in New Orleans, the end of the line, then catch another train going east to Bay Minette."

"I'm getting off in New Orleans." Sam speaks up out of his shyness. Sam is fifteen, stocky and dark, with his black wiry hair cut close to his scalp. He wears black slacks and a light blue button-down shirt with black musical notes on it.

"What's in New Orleans?" Stella asks Sam, making conversation.

"I got into a three-week summer class for jazz musicians. I play piano, trumpet and guitar and I have my trusty harmonica with me." His long fingers pull the instrument out of his shirt pocket.

"Cool! Play us something," says Stella, smiling.

Sam starts blowing into the harmonica cupped in his hands. The bluesy music fills the café car, and everyone hums along.

"That's really cool," Gino says, sweeping his long black hair across his face like a wave. Gino is sixteen and his warm brown eyes hide behind thick black eyeglasses, against his olive brown skin. He is wearing jeans and a turtleneck sweater, smelling of a musky cologne. "I'm heading for New Orleans also, then transferring to another train to Chicago. My aunt and uncle own an Italian restaurant there. I'm going to work for them this summer and earn some money before going back to school. I want to go on to college, but it's so expensive, and my parents don't have the money. So, God helps them who help themselves."

"Yeah, ya gotta meet God halfway," Sam says, and everyone snickers.

"Hey, you guys, wanna play some cards? Crazy eights? Twenty-one? War?" Joanne says.

"I got a bag of pretzels we can use for chips," Janet chimes in.

"Sounds fun," says Gino.

"I'm in," says Sam.

"We'll be getting off soon, so we're gonna go back to our seats and get our stuff together," Ronnie says.

So, five of the seven break out the cards, staying up all night playing cards for pretzels.

Then Janet and Joanne get off in Houston, while Gino, Sam and Stella ride the train to the end of the line that night. In New Orleans, a van from the music school comes to pick up Sam, while Gino and Stella wait in the train station until morning for their connection.

Gino boards his train traveling north for Chicago, and Stella takes the train going east at six in the morning. Another hour on the train and Stella's aunt will pick her up at the Bay Minette depot in her Cadillac de Ville.

Chapter 21

"Stella! Stella, over here," shouts a middle-aged woman waving her hand in the air. Her blonde permed hair glistens in the bright sunlight. Her blue and white check cotton top over blue jeans gives her a youthful appearance. Stella remembers her mother, Dotty, telling her, Helen followed her to Chicago to get away from the farm. Working for years as a housekeeper for a rich newspaper man, Mr. Huff, she managed to save her money to pay for beauty school. Then Helen went on to open a beauty parlor in Chicago. After many years, she sold the shop for a tidy sum and retired to her hometown, Bay Minette, Alabama.

"Oh! Hi, Aunt Helen. I made it," Stella says, waving back. Her aunt wraps Stella in a big, warm hug and plants a schmaltzy kiss on her cheek. Stella breaths in the sweet Alabama air, tasting so syrupy from the humidity and all the flowering trees and bushes close to the depot.

"Come on, you sweet thing, jump into my old Caddie. Your grandma can't wait to see Dotty's little girl. My, have you grown. You're almost a woman, wearin' a bra an' all."

Stella's face reddens under her freckles from the comment about her undergarments. She is only a size A cup stuffed with tissue paper to fill it out. Stella, at fourteen, is barely a hundred pounds, but already five foot four inches tall. Her thin arms poke out of her short-sleeved blouse, her plaid pedal-pushers hardly cover her knobby knees. She feels the awkwardness of her puberty, not a kid anymore, yet not a woman.

Why did my Aunt Helen have to point out my undeveloped figure? she thinks to herself. Getting into the Cadillac, she hunches her shoulders, folding her arms over her chest. Then changing the subject, Stella says to her aunt, "How far to Grandma's house?"

"Not far. About a half hour. Now buckle up your seat belt. Safety first!" her aunt says, turning to look at Stella. Helen puts the keys in the ignition and starts up the old Cadillac. Shifting the car into gear, she puts her foot down on the gas pedal and takes off with a squeal of the tires on the gravel parking lot and onto the paved road.

They drive out on a two-lane highway, lined with pine trees on both sides of the road reaching up to the sky. Crossing a small bridge, Stella looks out the window below to see a little stream bubbling over rocks, surrounded by lots of vegetation.

"Hey, Aunt Helen, what's this river here we're crossing?"

"It's Dyas Creek, darlin'. Creeks in these parts, kind of wander all over, springing up from ground water. There's plenty of wetlands around here. It rains so much, the water seeps into the ground and when the ground can't hold any more water, it comes to the surface and runs to the lowest part of the of the land, then forms ponds or lakes. That's just how it is 'round here."

About a half a mile further, they turn down a dirt road into the forest. The trees on either side of the dirt road stretch so tall, their top branches touch, forming an archway of greenery. At the end of the road is a weathered old barn and wooden fence with a gate.

Stella's aunt stops, gets out and unlatches the gate. Swinging the gate wide, the rusty hinges creak and moan. Then she drives the car through the gate and to the metal windmill used to pump water from the ground. She stops in front of the farmhouse, a blue-grey wooden structure with a screened in porch the length of the house. A four-foot-tall wooden fence separates the front yard from the forest. Red roses grow wildly up the side of the house, competing with the cement stairs and wooden handrail. Now, to Stella's surprise, there is running water in the kitchen and a bathroom in the house, not just the wooden outhouse in the front yard.

Helen gives the horn a 'toot, toot' and Grandma Margaret comes running out of the house in her floral housecoat, to greet her granddaughter from California. After giving birth to seven children, Margaret is a pudgy little old lady with her long brown wavy hair wound up in a bun on the back of her head. Her cotton dress comes to her ankles and covers her swollen puffy legs, suffering from poor circulation. Her wrists are deformed from hard field work, pulling a plow behind their mule. But her bright pink lipstick shows off her new false teeth behind her lips. Margaret is in good spirits because she has Dotty's little girl for the summer.

"Lordy, Lordy! Look at this girl. Stella looks just like her mother, Dotty, when she was that age. Get on over here, Stella, and give me some sugar!" Grandma Margaret says, grabbing Stella in her arms and hugging her tightly. When she finally lets go of her, she says "Now tell me, Stella, how's your mother?"

"Mama's fine," Stella says shyly, not knowing what else to say. She wasn't getting along with her mother lately. She resented all the chores her mother required of her, while her older brother does nothing but bring his friends over to tease her. She was so glad to get away from it all, at least for the summer, maybe forever.

"Well now, you come on in, Stella, and I'll show you around. We can talk later," Grandma Margaret says, taking Stella by the hand. Her aunt follows behind, carrying Stella's bags. "Now, Stella, you'll share this room with your Aunt Helen," her grandma says, showing Helen's room. "Ya must be tired from the long train ride. If ya want to take a little nap, that's okay too. Just make yourself at home and settle on in. I best be fixin' supper for ya."

Stella nods, and then as soon as her grandmother leaves, she flops down on the colorful patchwork quilt covering the big double bed and soon falls asleep.

Chapter 22

The sun is setting, casting red and golden rays on the horizon. The air is sticky and warm from the humidity of the afternoon. Stella awakens to the smell of fried chicken coming from the kitchen. She feels her stomach grumbling. She walks into the kitchen to see her Grandma Margaret at the stove cooking up some cornbread and speckled butter beans with little bits of bacon in it to bring out the flavor, a big pile of crispy fried chicken sits on a blue platter in the middle of the table. Sitting at the table in a wooden oak chair is her Aunt Helen, talking to Margaret in a low voice. The slant of Helen's eyebrows tells Stella, something is wrong.

"Did you hear, what's happenin' in Birmingham, Mama?" Helen asks as she lines the pie pan with vanilla wafers.

"No. What?" Margaret replies, piling up the yellow cornbread on another blue plater with tiny flowers painted around the edge of the plate.

"Some Negros want to change the laws up in Birmingham. They want to sit in the same waiting rooms as the Whites in the bus stations," Helen says while slicing up bananas to cover the wafers.

"So? What's the big deal?" Grandma Margaret says, combining sugar, cornstarch, and milk together in a pot to boil up some pudding.

"Well, the Whites don't like it. They got the police to put them in jail. Now the Negros are threatening to sue the city and there's a big ruckus," Helen says, now layering the bananas on top of the vanilla wafers.

"Oh Lordy. That don't sound good, even if it is away up north. Most folks down here in the southern part are as poor as most Negros and pay them no mind. When they gonna learn we is all God's children," Margaret says, shaking her head in disgust.

Now Margaret takes out three eggs and separates the yokes from the whites. She drops the yokes into the pot of pudding and the whites into a deep bowl. Margaret continues stirring the pot of pudding until bubbly, then she pours the pudding over the bananas and wafers. She places another layer of bananas and wafers and then again pours some more pudding over the second layer of bananas and wafers. She adds some sugar to the whites, and a teaspoon of vanilla, and beats long and hard with a hand crank beater until soft peaks form. She covers the whole banana pudding pie with the whipped-up meringue and pops it into the hot oven for a few minutes. When she pulls it out the meringue has turned from fluffy white to golden brown.

"Wow, Grandma Margaret, that's beautiful! What is it?" Stella's eyes pop wide open to take in the look of the creation, and the kitchen fills with the aroma of the vanilla and banana dessert.

"Stella, that's my famous banana pudding I made, just for you, my dear," Margaret says with a big toothy smile.

"Yum!" Stella replies, thinking of the tasty dessert.

"Did you have a good nap, Stella?" Helen asks, her face lighting up as she sets the table for dinner.

"Why, yes I did. Say, what were you and Grandma Margaret talking about when I came in the kitchen? It sounded serious," Stella asks, sitting down at the table.

"Oh, something happening in Birmingham, way up in northern Alabama. Nothing concerning us down here in the southern part of the state," Helen says, glossing over the news. She lays the white porcelain plates on the red and white checkered tablecloth then places silverware and napkins beside each plate.

Margaret pours the butter beans into a blue serving bowl then places it in the middle of the table with the chicken and cornbread. Finally, she sits down at the table.

"Let's say grace," Margaret says, as she folds her hands and bows her head. "Dear Lord, bless this food we are about to eat…"

A warm feeling comes over Stella's whole being. She is particularly thankful, thinking back over her journey across the country to a grandmother and aunt she barely knows, to be so welcomed by part of her expanded family. She fills her plate with southern fried chicken, butter beans and cornbread. She eats every delicious crumb, the flavors melting on her tongue, but she saves room for dessert, the luscious banana pudding.

After dinner, the dishes washed up, the three generations of women retreat to the screened in porch and talk for hours. Stella and Helen sit, swinging gently, on the wooden porch swing, suspended by two chains attached to the ceiling. Margaret sits comfortably in her favorite rocking chair. The night sky is filled with stars and the woods around the farmhouse sing with crickets and toads chirping out their mating calls.

Stella's eyelids start to droop as her head nods, bowing to her need for sleep. A yawn escapes her mouth before she can stifle it.

Her aunt smiles and says to her niece, "Looks like someone is ready for bed. Go along, Stella, we have a busy day tomorrow. I'm teaching you to milk a cow."

"A cow! All right!" Stella says, perking up a bit. "Sounds fun."

Chapter 23

The sun is rising and a rooster crows under Stella's bedroom window. She sits up in bed, groggy, rubs the sleep from her eyes and squints at the alarm clock on the oak dresser.

"Oh, only five o'clock," she moans, then flops back in bed, dropping her head on the feather pillow and covering her head with the hand-made quilt.

"Are you up, sweetie?" her aunt says, cracking the door open a bit, peeking into the bedroom. "We've got lots to do today. So, get your little hindquarters out of bed and get your clothes on. Grandma's in the kitchen fixin' breakfast."

Stella staggers out of bed, strips off her pajamas and slips into her pink undies. She grabs her white cotton bra, size 32A and fastens the hooks in front, then spins it around her chest and adjusts it to fit her small frame. *Wish I had more up front to fill in this bra,* Stella thinks to herself as she stuffs some tissue into the cups to fill it out. Then she pulls on a flowered pullover top and climbs into her blue capri pants, zipping them up on the side. She smells bacon frying and follows her nose to the kitchen. Standing by the white gas stove, her grandmother, only five feet tall, is frying up bacon and eggs.

Her grandmother has on a blue and green striped cotton housecoat that snaps up the front. Her light brown hair is wound up in a bun pinned to the back of her head as usual.

"Good morning, Stella. Did ya sleep good last night?"

"Yes, Grandma."

"You hungry, girl?" Her grandmother asks.

"Oh yes, Grandma. Everything smells really good."

"You just sit yourself right down here, darlin'. I'll fix you up a nice plate of country breakfast," her grandmother says. She brings Stella a white china plate of fresh scrambled eggs, crisp bacon and home-made biscuits. Stella never liked breakfast, but she can't resist the aromas coming from her plate. The taste of the flavorful fresh eggs, salty bacon and fluffy biscuits brings a smile to her lips. Breakfast never tasted this good.

Stella's aunt sits down beside her in front of her own plate of bacon and eggs. "Ya know, Stella, the scrambled eggs are fresh from our own chickens. That's why they're so tasty. They haven't been sitting in the market for days and days," Helen says, taking a forkful. "Eat up, Stella, we've got a lot to do today."

"Oh yeah? So, what's up today?" Stella says, taking her last bite of eggs, then smearing her biscuits with butter and homemade blackberry jam.

"Well, first we've got to feed the chickens and collect the eggs from the hen house. Then I'm going to show you how to milk old Betsy and put some fresh straw down in the barn. After we finish our chores, we'll drive to town and get some groceries. There's an ice cream store in town, we can get a cone or a sundae, even though it is only Tuesday."

"Ha-ha. Very funny," Stella says when her aunt snickers.

"Have you ever milked a cow, Stella?" her aunt asks, carrying her plate to the sink.

"Well, no. Is it hard?" Stella asks, sinking her teeth into the fresh biscuit with butter and jam. The tangy sweetness of the blackberry jam takes her by surprise. *Yum, this taste better than any candy I've bought from the store,* she thinks to herself.

"Well, no. milking cows is very soft, but it takes rhythm. You'll see," her aunt says, then asks, "You finished with breakfast?"

"Yes, Aunt Helen."

"Then bring me your plate so I can wash up the dishes and get on with our chores."

Stella carries her dishes to the sink as her grandmother smiles at the young girl, remembering Dotty at that age. How much she looks like her mother, tall and thin and all elbows and knees. She remembers brushing Dotty's hair, the same color as Stella's. She misses her oldest daughter, Dotty, since she moved to California, so far away. But what a treat it is to have Dotty's daughter come for the summer.

As Stella and her aunt leave the house for the barn, Aunt Helen cautions Stella about snakes. "Now, Stella," she says, "first scatter the chicken feed outside the coop and when the chickens come to eat, you can go in and gather their eggs. Just remember to look in the nests before putting your hand in to feel for eggs. Sometimes coral snakes and rattlers sneak into the hen house to eat the chickens' eggs.

"Yikes! Really?" Stella squeaks in a high-pitched voice.

"Yes, really. Now, after you finish with the chickens, come into the barn and I'll show you how to milk the cow. I'm going to let her calf nurse a while so the milk will come down. Sometimes old Betsy holds back her milk for her calf."

"Okay!" Stella says, heading for the chicken coop. Humming a little tune, she is happy to help with the farm chores. She loves the smell of the warm moist air surrounding her.

She watches her aunt lead old Betsy to her calf, and it suckles a while at one of its mother's long nipples. Stella ponders. *How different it is from the city. If you need eggs and milk, you just walk to the grocery store and buy it.* Helen then shoos the calf away and leads old Betsy back to the barn into her stall. There she ties the cow up to the stall and sets a metal bucket under her and sits down on a little three-legged stool. She washes Betsy's long teats with warm soapy water she brought in the bucket then throws the rest of the water out. Now she takes one of the teats between her thumb and forefinger and pulls down, grabbing another teat with her other hand and pulling down. Alternating hands, she pulls in rhythm, one then the other, as the milk comes out in a stream into the empty bucket, making a tinny sound.

Stella finishes scattering the chicken feed on the hard-grassless ground and the red and black feathered birds scurry around picking at the feed. She watches them compete for the seeds, frantically running around every which way and laughs at their antics. Then she walks into the dark, dank hen house and looks carefully into each straw nest on the shelves attached to the walls a few feet above the straw covered dirt floor. In each nest, she sees one or two perfectly oval eggs and gently lifts each one into her basket. Her fingers feel the coarse hard shell that is still warm. *The chicken must have just laid this one,* she thinks. *Yuk, this one still has some chicken poop on it. Well, guess we'll have to wash these eggs before we put them in the fridge.* After visiting each nest, her basket is full.

Stella walks into the barn to show her Aunt Helen her basket full of eggs and sees her sitting beside their cow on the little stool. She hears the steady rhythm of the milk squirting into the pail, half full now.

"Hey, Stella, want to try?" her aunt says, not missing a beat.

"Well... uh," Stella says, hesitating at the prospect of squeezing milk out of a cow.

"It's not hard. Sit down here and I'll show you," her aunt says. Her pail is almost full, so she cocks her head and looks at Stella and says, "Then just watch and you can try tomorrow."

"It's a deal." Stella surrenders to her aunt's persistence.

They gather up the eggs and milk and head toward the house. "Your grandma will wash the eggs and put the milk up in bottles, then put them in the fridge. We'll make a list of things we need then go to town. Okay Stella?"

"Okay!" Stella agrees with a big smile. "Can't wait."

Chapter 24

By mid-morning, the temperature is in the eighties, the blue sky is filling with white puffy cotton clouds and the humidity feels steamy. Stella begins to sweat in her aunt's baby blue Cadillac de Ville and rolls down the window on her side, letting a breeze blow in. Helen starts the powerful V-8 engine and shifts it into gear. Soon they are cruising down the highway at top speed heading toward Bay Minette. In half an hour, the big blue Caddie pulls into the Winn Dixie parking lot.

Stella and Helen enter the only supermarket in the area. By now the temperature is in the nineties and the fluffy white clouds have transformed into dark grey storm clouds, ready to dump rain and flash with lightning and thunder. Inside, Winn Dixie is cooler from the huge white metal fans circulating the air from the ceiling high above.

Pushing the wire framed shopping cart, Stella follows her aunt first to the fresh produce section. She sees the shiny rainbow colors of oranges, apples, peaches, plums and grapes in their bins. Then she sees the giant watermelons and tugs on her aunt's arm and says, "Auntie, can we get a watermelon?" Her eyes open wide, she smiles from ear to ear.

"Sure, sweet thing. Anything you like." Helen reaches into the big cardboard bin holding the massive green watermelons and starts thumping them until she hears the right resonating sound and says, "This one sounds like a good one, don't ya think, Stella?"

Stella nods her approval.

Helen then picks out some oranges, peaches and plums. She can tell if the peaches and plums are ripe by their sweet smell and tender touch. "I like to buy my fruit here because it's all locally grown," she explains, then she picks up a head of lettuce for salad to go with their homegrown tomatoes and peppers.

"How about some corn, Auntie," Stella says, eyeing a display of corn on the cob.

"We've got fresh corn and beans in our garden at home," her aunt replies.

"Oh."

"Now, let's see what looks good at the butcher counter," Helen says, walking to the back of the store, Stella following with the cart.

While Helen chooses meats for the week, Stella sees two water fountains on the wall next to the restrooms. She walks up for a closer look and notices a sign on one that says, 'WHITE' and the other one says, 'COLORED'. Curious, Stella turns on the 'colored' water and her aunt looks over at Stella and shouts, "No Stella, don't drink from that fountain!"

"Why not, Aunt Helen? I want to see what color the water is."

"No, Stella. It's for the 'Colored' people, the Negroes," her aunt whispers.

"You mean they get prettier water then the rest of us? Why?" Stella asks.

"Truthfully, I have no idea. Growing up here in Alabama in the Depression, there was no segregation here that I ever saw. We were all as poor as the Negroes. There was no money when the banks went broke and if our neighbors needed food, it didn't matter what color their skin was. We bartered and gave what we had. I was your age when I finished the eighth grade and was sent to Chicago to work. Grandma's sister, Ella, found me a job as a housekeeper for a rich newspaper man. For the last twenty-five years I've lived in Chicago, just moved down here in January. It's some sort of law to separate the Colored folks from the White folks here," Helen says, shrugging her shoulders at the mystery.

"Well, I think it's kind of strange. We don't do that in California and there are lots of black people, white people, brown people, all colors. It's just a skin color. In fact, people in California lay out in the sun to darken their skin and some color their hair." Stella laughs at the absurdity of it all.

Not wanting to make a scene, Helen hurries Stella along saying, "Come on, Stella, let's get our meat and a sack of sugar for your grandma to cook up her fruit preserves and get out of here. Say, we can get a quart of ice cream to take home, then we can share some with your grandma. What do you say?"

"Sure, that's a good idea, but can we get some chocolate sauce to go on top?"

"Absolutely, my dear niece!" Helen says with a smile.

Then Helen turns to the butcher behind the counter, dressed in white shirt and pants with a blood-stained white apron. Her voice is almost lyrical as she says, "Sam, would you be so kind as to wrap up a pound of your thick sliced bacon for me?"

"Yes, ma'am, Miss Helen."

"Oh, and also two pounds of that Angus ground beef, three of those pork chops over there and a pound of your smoked sausage."

"Why yes, Miss Helen, I'll get that there for you right away," Sam says smiling back, as he picks out her order. He wraps each one in brown butcher paper and writes the contents on the outside of the paper package. Then reaching over the counter, he hands Helen her purchase, pausing to gaze into her deep blue eyes. Sam is sweet on Miss Helen and wants to ask her out on a date.

"Thank you kindly, Sam. See you next week," Helen says with a smile.

Searching for the right words, Sam stammers, "Oh Miss Helen…"

"Yes, Sam?"

"Uh… do you like to fish?" Sam asks timidly.

Helen hesitates at the question, wondering where it is going, tilting her head to one side.

"Uh…well, Miss Helen… I have a long boat down by my place by the Tensaw River… and I'm uh… I'm takin' it out … on the river, fishin' Saturday night. There's mighty good fishin' on the Tensaw, when the sun goes down… Would you like to come along with me?"

Turning to her niece Helen says, "Stella, would you mind?"

"No, not really," Stella says raising her shoulders with a shrug.

Then turning back to Sam, she says, "Sure, Sam. Sounds fun," she tells Sam with a twinkle in her eye. Helen hasn't had a date since returning to Alabama in January. She loves to be on the water in the evening when the sun dips down into the horizon and turns the sky a mosaic of colors, framing the clouds with a silver lining. She is a country girl at heart and not afraid of hooking those wigglers on her line and dropping her hook in the water, waiting for the fish to bite.

"Then I'll pick you up at six, Saturday evening, Miss Helen," Sam says giving her a nod.

"See you soon, Sam," Helen says smiling.

"Always a pleasure, Miss Helen," Sam says, smiling back.

"Now, Stella, let's find that ice cream and a sack of sugar for grandma and head on home."

"And let's not forget the chocolate sauce, Auntie!"

As they leave the Winn Dixie, the skies open up and pour down rain. Stella and Helen make a run for the old

Caddie, holding their groceries tight to their chests to protect the paper sacks from the weather. If only they had the umbrella from the car. Feeling the rain soaking through their clothes, Helen starts up the car and turns on the windshield wipers to high speed for the first few miles. Then on the way home, as they cross over the Dyas Creek bridge, the rain lets up and blue skies show overhead. Stella is glad to get back to the farm.

***

What Stella did not know is that hundreds of miles north in Montgomery, Alabama, non-violent protests start in December of 1955, with a colored lady, Rosa Parks. She refused to give up her seat to a white man on the bus and is kicked off the bus. Her people boycott the bus lines and march for racial equality. For her act of civil disobedience, the forty-two-year-old seamstress from a local department store, is fired from her job and receives death threats years afterwards.

Chapter 25

Every day after morning chores, Helen takes her niece on a new adventure. After milking old Betsy, feeding the chickens and gathering eggs, Helen tells Stella of the day's escapade.

"Do you have a bathing suit, Stella?"

"No. Why?"

"We're going to the old swimming hole in the Perdido River, behind your Uncle John's farm," Helen says on the way back to the farmhouse with milk and eggs.

"But I..." Stella stutters.

"That's okay. You can wear one of mine. Might be a little big, but it will do," Helen says. Then going through her dresser drawers, she pulls out a one piece black and white striped suit. "How about this one?"

"Well... okay," Stella says, taking the bathing suit into the bathroom to try it on. "Ugh! It's too big," she moans. "Do you have anything smaller?"

"Oh, come on out here and let's see." Helen encourages her niece to come and model the oversized swimsuit. Stella is embarrassed by the loose-fitting garment that is clearly several sizes too large on her small frame.

When Stella finally comes out of the bathroom, she sees her aunt already wearing a one-piece solid black swimsuit. *For an old woman of forty, she looks surprisingly good,* Stella thinks. Her aunt is tall but shapely and her swimsuit fits every curve. With her hair cut short, permed, and colored a strawberry blonde, and her toenails and fingernails painted bright red, she is a real eye-catching beauty.

"Don't worry, Stella. We can tighten the suit up with a few safety pins for the day. Come on over here and I'll fix you right up." So, Helen does a little magic with safety pins and Stella looks halfway glamorous. "Now let's grab a couple of towels and we'll be off."

Climbing into the old Caddie, Helen turns to Stella and tells her, "Did you know when your mother and I were kids, your grandpa used dynamite to blow a hole in the river so we could swim and dive in it? It's really shallow and the other side of the river is Florida. You can actually swim over to Florida."

"Amazing!" Stella's eyes widening, hearing the little bits of history about her family. While listening to her aunt, she combs her hair into a ponytail and wraps it with a rubber band to keep it in place.

"We're going to swing over to your Uncle Billy's house and pick up a couple of your cousins, Joey and David. Then we will stop by your Uncle John's house and pick up your cousin, Johnny, before we hit the river. Deal?"

"Deal!" Stella says. She is excited to meet other kids in the family.

Joey is four years younger than Stella, but already as tall as she is. At ten years old, he is tall and thin with light brown hair and clear blue eyes. His high cheek bones and big toothy smile remind Stella of his dad, her Uncle Billy. He is a spirited youth who can climb trees and ride motorcycles.

His brother, David, is two years younger and much shorter and stockier. His straight white-blond hair hangs in bangs over his forehead and frames his face. David is shy and careful in what he says, if he says anything. He looks up to his big brother, Joey, and follows him wherever he goes. Both boys are barefooted with only cut-off jeans, each carrying a white towel.

Johnny is only five years old, short, and wiry. His dark brown hair is cut short in a no-nonsense style. He wears black swim trunks down to his knees and grips his faded blue towel tightly in his small hand. He is tough for a little guy and can climb trees with the best of them. Being a strong swimmer, he can swim across the Perdido River with no help at all.

After picking up Johnny, the three boys squeeze in the back of the old Cadillac and Stella rides in the front seat with her aunt. With her car full of kids, Aunt Helen heads down Hack Road to the very end then down a dirt road to the river. At the river Stella sees two girls in the water and three teenage boys on horseback riding through the woods on the Florida side. The boys dismount and tie their horses to one of the trees along the bank. Then they strip off their jeans and tee shirts down to their unders' and jump in the water.

The day is heating up and the clear blue sky starts forming puffy white clouds as the humidity fills the air. The area is surrounded by tall pines and scrub brush on both sides of the blue-green river and the sandy golden banks are easy on bare feet. Stella's cousins make a run towards the rushing river to escape the heat as she carefully walks down the bank with her aunt.

"Hey, man, we're here first," Joey says, challenging the teenage intruders, even though they are clearly older. Joey is spunky for his age and never backs down from an encounter.

"Say, punk, this river is big enough for all of us!" Dan, the taller of the three boys, yells back. With his stubby fingers, he rakes back his long brown hair, hanging over his eyebrows. Dan's mother is a good Christian woman who reprimands his temper. "Make peace instead," she always says.

"Yeah. Let's not fight over the river," Billy, the smaller teen says.

"Yeah, unless it's a water fight," Bubba, the stocky one says with a gleam in his green eyes, as he swings from an old rope in a nearby oak tree and flies into the crystal-clear water.

"All right! You're on!" says Joey and the water starts flying in all directions. Even the girls join in the water fight.

Everyone is thoroughly soaked, splashing each other in the blistering hot sun, and they all start laughing until their sides hurt. Stella watches the fun sitting on the bank with her toes in the water, when she spots something long and slithering through the water.

"Snake!" She yells, and the boys stop laughing and give the snake a wide birth as it glides down the Perdido River. Stella is surprised at the wildlife at the river, all minding their own business. *It seems,* she ponders, *the snakes are more afraid of us than we are of them.*

"Say, what's your name? I haven't seen you around these parts. Who are you?" Dan says, directing his questions to Stella.

Joey speaks up for Stella saying, "This here's our cousin, Stella. She's from California. She's staying with my grandma and aunt for the summer at the old farmhouse on Route 2."

Stella's face turns red as her red hair, as she tries to find words to say. "Uh… hi."

"California, huh? That's a long way from here. What's it like in California, Stella?" Dan has never been out of his own neighborhood, let alone knows anyone from another state. He wonders why anyone would want to come to Alabama in the hot humid summer.

"Well, I'm from Los Angeles, California which is in the southern part of the state. I live in the city, much different from Southern Alabama. Much different. In Los Angeles we don't have any rivers or creeks to swim in. If you want to go swimming, you have to drive all the way to the coast to swim in the Pacific Ocean. Or on a hot day in the summer, you can go to a swimming pool in the park or at the high school," she says, kicking her feet in the water.

"Girl, you sure talk funny... uh, I mean different. Can you slow down a bit? It's hard to understand what you're saying," Dan says to Stella, cocking his head to one side at the girl from the west coast.

"Sure, Dan. Say, I have a question for you. Why do you have separate drinking fountains for Colored people? What's the deal? In Los Angeles we have lots of Colored people and we don't have separate drinking fountains for them. In fact, we have lots of Mexicans and lots of Chinese and a mix of people, but we don't give them their own drinking fountains," Stella asks, lifting her palms skyward.

"I don't really know. We don't have that many Negroes in these parts. I see them when we pick cotton for the Hadleys over in Atmore. The Colored folk can pick far more cotton than me and my brothers. In fact, my mama sends us out early in the morning while the dew is still on them cotton balls just because they are heavier when they're wet and we get more money per sack, being as we're paid by the poundage," Dan tells Stella, while treading water in the deeper part of the river.

"So, the Coloreds are not around here?" Stella asks.

"Well, no, not really. They have their own neighborhoods. They're as poor as us White folks. They

127

just work like all of us. But from time to time, I'll see Ole Black Tom riding his big chestnut stallion to town. He works for the Hadleys full time. He's their foreman and oversees the crops. He knows everything to know about cotton," Dan says, then dives into the water headfirst and swims to the other side of the river and climbs up the bank. "Got to go pretty soon. We got to get back home and finish our chores before dinner or Mama will whip us good."

"See ya, Dan," Stella shouts across the river.

"See ya," Dan shouts back, pulling his jeans and tee shirt on. He and his two friends mount their horses and ride back through the woods.

Stella puzzles over the differences in South Alabama, trying to make sense of it all. At fourteen years old, she never heard of such things as separating people by color. In a few years she will see it all played out on news stations on television.

Chapter 26

After the three boys leave on horseback, Joey says to Stella, "Hey, cous', do you know these woods are haunted?"

"Now, Joey," scolds Aunt Helen. "Don't you go scarin' your California cousin."

"It's true," intrudes Sally Sandburg, the smaller of the two girls swimming in the river. "My granddady tells me your grandma saw it, a ghost, coming out of the woods. Your grandma, she was so scared, she fainted."

"I was told the same thing and to stay out of the woods at night," says Rita Ryan, the taller girl. Sally and Rita are best friends, growing up together. Their parents are neighbors to the Pimperls, and their grandparents settled on the same farmland with the Pimperls in the 1920s.

"Aunt Helen, do you remember what happened? Did grandma really see a ghost?" Stella asks turning to her aunt.

"I was just a child when it happened... But I do remember grandma was pregnant and fainted," her aunt admits. "And I remember your mother, Dotty, running to get one of the neighbors, I think it was Jim Ryan."

"See, Stella. Just ask Grandma Margaret. She'll tell you the whole story," Joey remarks knowingly. His little brother, David, nods in agreement.

As the sky clouds up with thunderheads, lightning streaks though the air, then a loud clap of thunder. Heavy raindrops begin to fall from the heavens. Taken by surprise, Stella lets out a loud scream from the flash of lightening and the sound of the rolling thunder. She feels a little foolish for screaming, but California rarely has thunderstorms like this.

Helen looks up at the sky and says, "Let's get out of the water and head for shelter. It's unsafe to be on the water during a thunderstorm. Rita, Sally, do you need a ride home?" Helen offers the girls.

"Oh, that would be great, Miss Helen," Sally says as the rain dumps. They all make a run for the car.

"Okay, all of you, pile in the old Caddie. Quick! It's pouring." Helen barks out the command like a general directing soldiers. Joey, David and all the girls crowd into the back seat and Johnny takes the front seat next to his aunt. Johnny is the first one to be dropped off on Hack Road. Then driving down Highway 31, Helen takes a left on Route 2 and swings by Joey and David's house. They make a run for their front porch, dodging the rain as best they can. Helen then drives by the Ryan's house to let Rita off. Now the rain is slowly easing up. By the time Helen reaches the Sandburg's house to drop off Sally, blue sky is braking out behind the clouds. Now home at the Pimperl's farmhouse, a rainbow bends across the sky, even though the roads are all muddy from the downpour.

Home at last, Stella walks up the stairs to the porch and as she opens the front door, the smell of fresh baked peach cobbler and fried catfish meets her. She hears her grandmother in the kitchen shuffling about, cooking up something good, and the clink of dishes as she sets the table for dinner.

Stella dashes into the bedroom to change out of the wet swimsuit her Aunt Helen let her use and into a pair of pink pedal pushers and pink striped blouse. She combs her red wavy hair out of the ponytail and ties a pink scarf around her head, letting it fall to her shoulders to dry. Slipping on her canvas shoes, she begins to wonder about this ghost her cousin Joey talks about and if it is still here?

Walking into the kitchen, Stella sees the old wooden table covered with a white and yellow flowered linen cloth, white china plates set with silver forks and spoons on each side of the plates. In the middle of the table is a white platter piled high with crispy fried catfish, a white serving bowl of field peas and bacon, corn on the cob and a big platter of grandma's famous cornbread.

Stella serves herself a big helping of everything then grabs an ear of corn and sinks her teeth into the succulent kernels. "Yum, this is so good, Grandma."

Grandma smiles and nods her approval.

But all through dinner, Stella is thinking about the ghost that supposedly haunts the woods around Dyas Creek. Is it real or just an imaginary spirit that haunts the people around this area?

The Perseids meteor shower is coming up in August and Stella wants to see it on a clear night. But will it be safe? Or will there be some ghost or goblin to fear out there at night? Maybe she can ask her grandmother if the ghost is still lurking about or if it is okay to hang out late at night to watch the falling stars?

Chapter 27

Stella helps Aunt Helen wash up the dishes after dinner. Her auntie fills the yellow plastic dishpan with hot soapy water and one by one lowers the white china dishes in to soak. Carefully, she lifts each plate out of the water and uses an old cotton rag to rub the soapy water over the plates until clean. She repeats the routine with the rest of the dishes and stacks them in the grey metal sink. She then runs hot water over the dishes and one by one, hands them to Stella to dry with a clean, cotton dish towel, to stack on the cleared table so that Grandma Margaret can put them away in their proper place. This procedure of washing dishes is foreign to Stella.

Stella chuckles to herself.

"What's so funny, Stella?" her aunt inquires.

"Well, the kitchen in my house in California has a built in mechanical 'dishwasher' that does most of the work. At home, my mother does not trust me with her dishes. She's afraid I might drop and break one of her china plates. So, I never help her in the kitchen."

"Well, that's too bad. You can get plenty of practice out here on the farm," Helen replies.

Then they both go out to the screened in porch to watch the sunset. As the sky darkens with the fading rays of the sun, Stella sits on the old wooden porch swing watching the fireflies and dragonflies, flit about the warm summer air. The frogs and bugs start singing their night songs while Stella thinks about the possibility of spirits haunting the woods close to the farmhouse. She likes the safety of the screened in porch, but she longs to lay out in the tall grass out front and stare up at the stars in the dark sky. The stars are much brighter out in the country with no city lights to compete with them.

Stella's grandmother comes out to the porch with a ball of cherry red yarn, large knitting needles and slippers she is working on for Christmas. She settles into her rocking chair and starts clicking away at her knitting.

"Grandma…" Stella cautiously starts to ask.

"Yes, dear?"

"Do you believe in ghosts?"

"What?" her grandmother questions.

"Do you believe in ghosts? Are there ghosts around here?" Stella asks again.

"Where did you hear that, Stella? Have your cousins been trying to scare you by telling stories?" Her grandmother stops knitting to give Stella her full attention.

"Well, my cousin, Joey, tells me, you saw a ghost out here. Is it true?" Stella confesses, looking over to where the forest meets the fenced-in yard. The sun is setting and shadows from the lights in the farmhouse cast strange shapes from the trees in the forest.

"I've lived here at the edge of the woods for the past forty years..." her grandmother replies, wondering where this conversation is going. "Why do you ask, Stella?"

"Just wondering..." Stella says, nervously rubbing her folded arms to keep the chill off.

"Well, Stella," her grandmother continues, "some say the spirit of someone who has died never leaves the Earth until there is no one left to remember the one who died." Looking down at her red yarn on the needles, Grandma Margaret carries on knitting the Christmas slippers.

"Well, what about that old man who lived in the woods? Sally Sandburg said her grandpa told her you saw his ghost and fainted. Did you?" Stella presses on.

"Lordy, child. That was a long time ago," Grandma Margaret says with a catch in her throat. She feels the pain in her heart from the sadness of that night.

"His name was Gelsinger," Grandma Margaret continues with a sigh. "He was an old German man who lived at the edge of the woods near Dyas Creek. He would ride out here on his black stallion horse and bring me my mail whenever there was a letter from my sister in Chicago. Or when we'd order shoes or clothes from a catalog, he'd bring the packages from the post office in town down to the farm. He was a good man, but rough around the edges. He'd go on out to Dyas Creek after dark with a lantern and look for them old 'gators. Some're as much as ten feet long. Once he spotted them red glowing eyes, peeking above the murky water, he'd cruise on alongside of it and lasso its snout, then wrap that rope around its jaws so it couldn't snap. Then jump on its back and wrestle it like a bucking bronco, till he could slit its throat with his bowie knife. Lordy, I never known a man so fearless."

"Wow. He must have been really tough," Stella says, spellbound by the story.

"Yep. He was. But once he made a wrong move and got snapped in the leg by one of those old 'gators. Walked with a limp after that one. Ya know, he loved the fight, but he loved the money from the skins better. He would get two, three hundred dollars for the skins in Mobile or New Orleans. But he didn't believe in banks. He'd fill up them old mason jars full of gold and silver coins then bury them under his shack. Whenever he needed money to buy something, he'd just dig up one of those jars of money."

"Where did he get the jars, Grandma?" Stella interrupts.

"Well, when he'd bring me my mail, I'd give him a jar of my canned peaches from the summer. My, he sure loved my peaches. That's not all he loved. He was sweet on a little gal from New Orleans, a Creole gal, you know, a mix of Black and White. He'd bring her down to his place once or twice a week and she'd clean and cook for him and more. She disappeared after he was murdered. Probably went back to New Orleans."

"*Murdered*! What happened to Mr. Gelsinger, Grandma?" Stella questions her grandmother about the murder. She wants to know all the details.

"Well, it's said, in August 1924, a couple of rough-neck fellas heard Gelsinger got a good price for his alligator skins in Mobile. One day they followed old Gelsinger home through the woods and they waited till darkness covered the forest to make their move. The old man already put away his money, had a bite of leftover stew, and was enjoying a drink of his homemade hooch. When the two men broke into the shack, they demanded his money, pointing a hunting rifle at the old man's head. Well, that stubborn old man would not give them a cent of his money. Gelsinger grabbed the barrel of the rifle and bang! It went off, shooting the old man in the chest. The two robbers looked around Gelsinger's shack but could not find where the old man stashed his money. The old man started to move, and one of the two fellas broke the jug of hooch over Gelsinger's head. Then the other fella knocked the old man's lantern off the table and set fire to the brew that flowed over the floor. The little wooden shack went up in a blaze like a tinderbox. The fire could be seen for miles around. Old man Gelsinger died in the fire that burnt his house to the ground." Grandma Margaret looks to the sliver of the new moon and sighs. She lays down her knitting, no longer in the mood.

"Did the police or sheriff ever find the ones who killed Gelsinger?" Stella asks, her mouth hanging open, listening to her grandmother's tale.

"Why yes, darling." Margaret perks up. "They found the two culprits. They both got seven years hard labor. One of them, Ronnie Richmond, when he got out, he was a changed man. He found Jesus. Your Grandpa Pimperl gave him a job tapping turpentine from the pine trees in the forest back then. He eventually saved enough money to move on to Texas and work on the oil rigs in the Gulf."

"Does Grandpa still tap the pine trees for their sap?" asks Stella.

No, dear. Not after your grandpa bought the Blue Lantern store on Highway 31. He usually stays out there during the summer months.

"What about the money, Grandma? Did anyone ever find the jars of money?" Stella asks, her eyes wide with wonder, thinking of the old man's buried treasure.

"No. Many looked, but no one ever found the silver and gold coins Gelsinger hid in mason jars so long ago. It continues to be a mystery to this day," Grandma Margaret concludes. "Well, I'm all tuckered out telling you this story. It is getting late."

"But wait, Grandma. What about the ghost you saw? Is he still around, haunting the forest?" Stella asks, wanting to hear more.

"Well, I reckon. I saw it once when I was a young mother. He reached out at me one night trying to tell me something, but I was too scared. I just screamed and fainted." She doesn't want to talk about what happened that night. The memory of the stillbirth of her first baby boy is too painful to talk about, even after all the years.

"Have others seen his ghost?" Stella wants to know everything.

"Why yes. Your own mother, Dotty, saw the old man's ghost once, when she was a child in the woods, out there by the fence that separates the forest from the front yard. She was maybe your age, about thirteen or fourteen. That was several years after I saw him that night... Now, that's enough of that. It's way late and time for bed, Stella."

"Okay, Grandma." Stella jumps off the porch swing and follows Grandma into the house. Her thoughts are full of the story of Gelsinger and his ghost. And what about all that money hidden away in her grandmother's mason jars? Is it still out there, somewhere, or is it just a story?

Chapter 28

That night Stella dreams of walking along Dyas Creek where the pilings of the old bridge stick out of the water like hands reaching out of the deep. The banks of the creek are lined with tall grasses, scrubby bushes and thorny vines, tangled in pine trees like haunting spiderwebs.

In her dream, she sits on a fallen log and fishes in the creek, throwing her line far off, into the dark water. Her line gets snagged on something deep in the water. She pulls at the line, harder and harder, until it gives and pulls up a slender shadowy figure of an old man with a long white beard. He calls out "Margaret" and Stella drops her fishing pole; shock grasps her whole being at the sight of the ghostly figure. Fearlessly, Stella stands. Putting her hands on her hips she says, "Who, the heck, are you?"

"I... am... the ghost... of Gelsinger," the apparition says sluggishly.

Stella wants to scream or run away, but she gathers her wits about her and asks, "Why have you called out my grandmother's name?"

"Oh... if I could tell her..." The spirit pauses.

"Tell her what? What would you tell her? Tell me, Mr. Gelsinger's ghost. Tell me!"

Stella mumbles in her sleep, then wakes herself up. "Tell me," she says one more time and opens her eyes. "Wow, what a dream. It was so real."

Stella's aunt knocks on the bedroom door and sings out in her soprano voice, "Morning! Time to rise and shine, Stella. Your grandma has breakfast on the table. And, after our morning chores, I'll teach you how to ride Old Rex." Old Rex is Helen's old golden-brown horse she keeps in the barn.

"Really!" Stella is thrilled at the chance to ride Helen's horse. It looks so easy in the western movies. She once rode a pony at the county fair, but it was hooked up to a wheel with other ponies and just went around in a circle.

"Yes, dear girl, after breakfast and chores. And remember..."

"I know, look in the chicken nests before I put my hand in," Stella says, smiling back at her aunt.

Stella goes out to the henhouse to gather eggs, while Helen takes hold of their milk cow and leads her into the barn. There she ties up the cow to the stable where Betsy can feast on hay. Helen sets down the tin pail beneath the cow's udder and places the three-legged stool to the right of the cow. Now she starts her rhythmic squeeze-pull of the udders as the milk squirts into the bucket.

Stella enters the henhouse to collect the eggs, still thinking of her dream last night of the encounter with a ghost. She carelessly reaches into each nest to feel for eggs, picking them up to place in her basket. In the third nest she feels something that is not smooth and roundish. It feels rougher and more cylindrical. Her mind flashes back to reality.

"Ack!" she screams in her high-pitched voice, as a scaly creature occupying the hen's nest, slithers out onto the dirt floor of the henhouse.

"What the... What's going on Stella?" Helen yells out as the cow jerks loose, hearing Stella's scream. Old Betsy knocks over the milk pail, spilling milk out all over the straw covered barn floor and Helen's new leather boots.

"Snake!" Stella gasps, as she watches the five-foot long copperhead wind lazily out of the henhouse with a belly fat from eggs it's swallowed. Stella gives it a wide berth as it crawls on the hard ground past her.

"Jesus Lord almighty, girl. Didn't I tell you to always look in the nests before picking out the eggs? You could have been bitten. That one there is one of the poisonous snakes around here." Helen scolds her niece for her negligence in not paying attention.

"I'm sorry, Aunt Helen," Stella pleads, on the verge of tears.

"I lost all the milk as well. Your scream startled old Betsy. She kicked over the milk pail and spilled all the milk. Now we have none for the morning," Helen says angrily, giving Stella the stink-eye.

"Sorry..." Stella says, sticking out her lower lip for pity.

"What's done is done... No use crying over spilled milk," Helen sighs, then chuckles to herself over the phrase. "How many eggs did you get, Stella?"

"Four, but I dropped the basket and one rolled out and broke. I can go in and see if I missed any," Stella says, shyly, feeling like a silly city girl.

"Sure. Take a look. Then we'll take what we have back to the farmhouse."

"Do I still get to ride your horse, Aunt Helen?"

"Of course," Helen says with a smile.

"Yippie!" Stella says with glee, then goes back into the henhouse and finds two more eggs. Helen and Stella take what they have to the kitchen and tell Grandma Margaret all about the mornings activity and why they don't have milk for the morning.

Grandma wags her finger at Stella and says, "You be more careful, missy. Snake bites are not much fun."

Stella nods her agreement.

***

Later that day, Helen takes Stella out to the barn where Rex, a golden-brown quarter horse is kept. He is a gentle horse and fairly old, but skittish around strangers. Helen whispers softly to Rex, as she slips Rex's bridle over his face. Then tightening up the straps, she leads him outside and ties him to the fence post. Grabbing the heavy saddle nearby, she slings it over Rex's back. He flinches as the saddle settles into place. Now Helen pulls up and cinches the straps beneath his belly.

"There. He's ready. Now just put your foot in this here stirrup and swing your body into the saddle. Got it?" Helen says to Stella, holding Rex's bridle, stroking the horse's neck to keep him calm.

"Yep, I got it." Stella says confidently. She awkwardly swings her leg right over old Rex and lands on the hard ground. A little shaken, she gets to her feet, brushes herself off with as much dignity as she can muster.

"You can do it, Stella. Just give it another try," Helen encourages her niece.

Stella tries again, while Helen holds the horse still. After a few more times… success. Stella holds on tight and she is in the saddle, ready to ride.

"Wow, look at me, I am way up here!" Stella says, feeling the euphoria of sitting atop of a six-foot high horse. She wraps her legs around its middle and sits up straight. Holding onto the horn of the saddle with her right hand and the reins of the bridle with her left, she feels ten feet tall.

"Now, give Rex a little slack in the reins and kick his sides a little…" and away they go, trotting around the farmyard. After a few rounds, Stella feels like a real cowgirl, her confidence soaring. In her mind, she thinks it would be great to have a horse to get around.

Coming back around, her aunt takes hold of the reins and with a steady hand, helps Stella off the back of Old Rex. Once on the ground, Stella feels wobbly and bow-legged, but triumphant. She will write a letter to her mother in Los Angeles tonight, telling her about her horse-riding adventure. She is sure her brother will be so jealous.

Chapter 29

On Saturday afternoon, Helen starts primping for her date with Sam. Showering and washing her hair, she towels off her body and then wraps her blond curly hair in the towel. She wipes off the steam on the bathroom mirror and gazes at her reflection. Reaching for her beige pressed powder, she smooths it over her nose then cheeks and forehead until her face is all the same color. Carefully, she brushes a pinkish color on her cheeks to brighten her face. Then skillfully, she takes her pretty pink lipstick and lines her full lips with the color. Mashing her lips together, she then blots her lips on a tissue. Looking at herself again in the mirror, she is satisfied with the result.

Now Helen heads toward her bedroom and reaches into her bureau drawer and pulls out a bra and panties to match. She steps into the panties and slips into the bra, hooking it in the back. In her closet, she chooses dark blue pedal-pushers and a blue and white cotton polka-dot blouse that buttons up in front with short sleeves. She pulls up the pants and slips on the blouse, fastening all buttons except the top one, to show a little cleavage. Stepping into her white leather flats, she is ready. She glances at the clock on the wall and it reads quarter to six. Sam will be there in fifteen minutes. Just enough time to spray on a little Straw-Hat cologne on her neck and wrists. Aunt Helen comes out of the bedroom and says, "Now, Stella, no need to wait up for me."

"You'll be home late?" Stella questions.

"Why yes, missy. Sam and I are going out night fishing on the river. It's the best time to catch catfish, while the sun is setting, until dark."

"But Auntie, the Perseid Meteor Shower is tonight, and I want to see it. Can't I please go outside tonight after dark and watch the stars fall?"

"Grandpa is working the Blue Lantern tonight, so you'll have to check with Grandma Margaret. If it's okay with her, it's okay with me," Helen says, feeling a little hesitant.

"All right!" Stella says joyfully.

Sam drives up in his white Ford pickup and toots his horn. Helen runs out and hops in the front seat, waving goodbye to Stella.

***

Grandpa Pimperl's Blue Lantern is a little convenience store along Highway 31 where two gas pumps stand outside. Inside the little store there is a long counter and a few tall stools to sit at. An ice chest full of bottles of cold beer and soda pop sits in front of the counter on the wooden floor, for easy access. A smattering of other stuff like chips, peanuts and candy as well as canned goods and such, is stacked on the wooden shelves surrounding the room. Grandpa Pimperl has built a little room in the back of the store where he has a couch, a table and a hot plate to cook something up. Outside, in the back of the store, he grows his tomatoes, peppers and okra.

***

Later that night after dinner, Stella and Grandma Margaret sit on the screened in porch waiting for the stars to come out. Fireflies flit around in the woods, their little bottoms lit up, blinking in the dark. A giant ghostly moth with pale green wings as big as a man's hand, hugs the wooden door of the porch and cicadas sing out in the night.

"Grandma, can we sit outside under the stars?" Stella asks, wanting to get the full view of the meteor shower. She has never seen such a sight. In Los Angeles, there are so many city lights competing with the stars, only the brightest ones shine through the night, but only if there is no smog or fog blanketing the sky.

"We sure can, Stella. Let me go inside and get one of my old quilts to spread on the grass to lay on." Grandma Margaret goes inside for a few minutes and brings out a patchwork quilt of colorful patterns she made many years ago. It is well worn, but thick and soft so as the damp grass will not soak through.

"Stella, you best put a long sleeve shirt and long pants on before you go out. The mosquitos are hungry little old blood suckers, and they'll eat you up alive."

"Good thinking, Grandma," Stella says, dashing into the house to cover her long arms and legs. She does not want those big old itchy welts on her from their bites.

They go outside the protection of the screened in porch and into the night, spreading the quilt under an old magnolia tree in the front yard with a clear view of the sky. Laying on their backs they gaze upward.

"Now, you see there, that group of stars, that there is the Big Dipper," Grandma says, pointing up at the heavens in one direction.

"Oh, I see," says Stella, amazed at her grandmother's knowledge.

"And see how those stars line up, that is Orion's Belt," her grandmother says, pointing out the different constellations.

Just then, there is a streak of light that flashes through the sky. "There! Did you see that?"

"Yes! Is that one?" Stella says, excited at the sight of a shooting star.

"Why yes, indeed. Say, there's another one. The stars are falling in Alabama."

The two of them lay on their backs on the comfy quilt and count the meteorites whizzing by above their heads. Then, Stella hears something in the distance. She glances in the direction of Dyas Creek and sees a glimpse of something white, moving through the woods.

"Grandma! Look over there," pointing in the direction of the white flowing objects. "What is that? Is it... a ghost?" Stella says, feeling a chill run up her spine as she sits up to get a better look.

Grandma Margaret sits up and takes a look, then shakes her head. "Lord almighty. I didn't think they came this far south. We best be getting into the house. Don't want any trouble."

"Grandma, what is it?"

"The Klan," Grandma says abruptly and spits on the ground, disgusted by what she sees.

"The Klan? What's the Klan, Grandma?" Stella asks, puzzled by her grandmother's reaction.

"The Ku Klux Klan. They's a bunch of hateful old white men, who think they're better than anyone else. They be givin' the Colored folks a bad time. They've done some horrid things up north in Alabama and other states, too. They have no business around here. Let's go inside, just to be safe," Grandma Margaret says, as she and Stella stand. Then they lift the quilt at one end and give it a good shake before folding it.

"I think we've seen enough stars for tonight," Grandma Margaret says with a weary smile.

"Yes, Grandma, and a few fake ghosts, too," Stella says with a laugh.

Chapter 30

As time goes by, Sam changes his schedule in the meat department to the early morning shift, cutting meat for the day. He is done by noon. Now, Stella's Aunt Helen sees more and more of Sam and has less time for Stella. With Grandpa Pimperl at the Blue Lantern most days and Grandma Margaret busy cooking, cleaning, washing, and tending her kitchen garden, Stella finds herself trapped on the farm with no way out.

Desperate, Stella remembers the horse in the barn, Old Rex. She thinks to herself; *I could saddle up Old Rex and ride him down to the highway. There is a little store across the highway, Demco's, where we pick up the mail. They have lots of stuff there, like sodas, chips, and candy. I know how to saddle up Old Rex and ride him. It's not hard. Aunt Helen showed me.* Stella's confidence is growing. At fourteen years old, she thinks she can saddle up Rex on her own, ride him to the highway, and tie him up. Then run across the highway to check the mail, get some munchies, then cross the highway again and jump on Rex to ride him back to the farm. No one will ever know. Easy, so she thinks.

In theory, it is a simple plan. In actuality, well...

Aunt Helen takes off with Sam again for some sort of music concert down in Pensacola. She won't be back for a while.

Stella dresses quickly in blue jean shorts and a yellow top. She slips on her socks and white tennis shoes, tying her yellow laces tight. Stella shouts out, "Grandma, I'm going outside for a little while."

"That's fine, dear," Grandma Margaret answers back from the kitchen.

Now Stella runs out to the barn where the saddle and bridle hang near Old Rex. She grabs the bridle and strokes the horse's back before she slips the bridle on his head, then tightens up the straps. Lifting the heavy leather saddle, Stella slings it over the horse's back, as he starts to move away.

"Easy, Rex," Stella coos with a soft reassuring voice to calm the horse. She's seen this technique in the western movies. "Easy now. We're just going to go for a little ride, old boy."

Old Rex settles down and Stella cinches the saddle straps around Rex's enormous belly, then leads him out of the barn, holding the reins tight. Out in the open, still holding the reins, Stella inserts one foot into one stirrup and swings her other leg over the saddle. She feels for the other stirrup until she finds it with her other foot.

"There! I did it," Stella says, smiling broadly as she sits up straight in the saddle. She feels like the queen of the world, sitting high on top of a real horse. Cautiously, she nudges Rex on the sides with her heels and Rex starts to move, ever so slowly.

"Getty-up, old boy," she says flicking the reins a little and Rex trots a little faster. The gate is open, and Stella triumphantly trots out of the farm onto the dirt road that leads to the highway. She is on her way, just as she planned.

When she gets to the highway, Stella dismounts and ties the reins to a small tree. She gives Rex a little pat on the back and says, "Good boy, Rex. Now you stay here, and I will be right back."

After looking both ways, Stella dashes across Highway 31. Walking into the old wooden building, she sees Ray Demco behind the glass counter. "Hey there, missy. What can I do for you today?" Ray is tall and skinny in his plaid shirt and Levi overalls. His thick brown hair is turning grey at the sides. His heavy work boots are laced up to the top of his ankles. He and his wife, Wanda, have worked the store for years. The mail for route two is left at his store for those who live in the area.

"Hi! I'm Stella, John and Margaret Pimperl's granddaughter. My grandma," she lies, "sent me up here to pick up any mail."

"Hum... let me see..." Ray says. "Here's a catalog from Sears for Mrs. Pimperl." He pulls it from the pile of mail and hands it to Stella.

"Thanks. Oh… are there any letters for me, Stella Weiss?" she says, hoping for a letter from her mother in California.

Ray shuffles through the letters again but finds nothing else. "Nope. No other mail or letters. Sorry."

"Oh… okay," Stella says sadly, glancing at her shoes. Then reaching into her pocket she pulls out a dollar bill. "Uh… can I buy a soda pop?"

"Sure, little miss. What do ya want?" Ray smiles broadly, eying the spunky teenager.

"How about one of those Orange Nehi sodas. They look pretty good," Stella says, smiling back at Ray.

"Sure thing. Want to drink it now or later? I can take the bottle cap off for ya?"

"Sure. That'll be great," Stella says, watching Ray pry the cap off of the glass bottle of pop with a device bolted to the wall.

"Here you go, little lady. That'll be twenty-five cents." Stella hands Ray her dollar bill and he gives her back three quarters and the open bottle of soda.

Now with the Sears catalog under her arm and the Nehi in her other hand, she takes a swig of the sweet orange soda, feeling the cold drink run down her dry throat, quenching her thirst on the hot day.

"Thanks again," she says and leaves the store.

Waiting for the few cars and pickups to pass on Highway 31, Stella walks gingerly across the highway. When she gets to the other side, she does not see her horse tied to the small tree. Her mouth falls open, seeing only the bridle tied to the tree, but no horse. Looking around there is absolutely no horse in sight.

"Oh, no. I can't believe it," Stella cries, dropping the Sears catalog under her arm. "How can I be so stupid? Now what?" she says, blinking the tears away. "Guess I'll have to walk all the way back to the farm," she moans.

Untying the bridle from the small tree, and bending over to pick up the catalog, Stella resolves to start walking. The dusty red dirt road back to the farm is lined with pines and oaks. The wildflowers are blooming profusely after the pop-up rain showers in the afternoons. Butterflies of every color flitter about, sucking up nectar from the flowers in the woods. The air smells so fresh with all the oxygen released by flowers and trees along the way. Stella breathes in deeply the fragrance of the forest and smiles to herself. *What an amazing place this is*, she thinks.

After half an hour of walking, Stella sees the wooden gate to the farm. Beyond the gate, in the grassy pasture, she eyes Old Rex, head down, calmly munching on the green grass.

Chapter 31

By the dog days of August, the temperature soars to about one hundred degrees and the afternoon thunderstorms fill the air with humidity. Black asphalt streets transform the rain on the surface to steam, rising up in clouds of fog. Insect devouring pitcher plants along the side of the roads trap their prey in their white tubular leaves with a sweet sticky goo at the bottom of their pitcher. Black flying lovebugs swarm searching for a mate, attach to the opposite sex and secrete blue slime that sticks on all surfaces.

Stella is bored, looking into the bathroom mirror as she combs her long red hair into a ponytail. She longs for the cool Pacific Ocean back home in California. *If only my aunt was not so busy with her boyfriend, Sam,* Stella ponders. *Aunt Helen is gone again and who knows when she will be back. If only I could get off the farm, but Grandma doesn't drive, and Grandpa is already at the Blue Lantern. It's so hot today, but there is no way to get to the creek and go swimming.*

She thinks about escaping on Old Rex to Dyas Creek and taking a swim in the sweltering humid weather but recalls her attempt at riding Rex to the highway. Shaking her head, she remembers walking back to the farm after Rex freed himself from his tether.

She hears that the local boys jump off the bridge over Dyas, but she is not that brave. Besides, it is a long way back from the highway and an even longer way back from Dyas Creek.

"Wait…" Stella whispers out loud, "If I could walk all the way home from the Demco's when Old Rex deserted me, I can walk to the highway from the farm. No biggie." Stella sits down on her bed and pulls on her socks and sneakers, tying her laces tight.

Quietly, she tiptoes out of the farmhouse and starts walking down the dirt road toward the highway. Stella swells with pride as an independent woman, walking fast, her back straight as a board, determined to see more of Alabama than her grandparents' farm.

When Stella reaches the highway, she thinks, *I could walk to the Blue Lantern, Grandpa's store. It's not so far and I'm a strong walker. I've walked further than that back home, walking to and from school.*

As Stella walks down Highway 31 towards her grandfather's store, an old blue Chevy pickup truck pulls up beside her and stops. An old man in coveralls yells out the window, "Where ya goin', little lady?"

"I'm going to the Blue Lantern up the highway," Stella yells back to the old man.

"It's a mighty far walk for a little lady like you. Wanna ride?"

"Sure," Stella says, not thinking any harm in accepting a ride from the old man.

"Hop right on in," the old man says with a crooked smile as he gives a tip of his blue baseball cap. His thin face is lined with deep creases and covered by a dark grubby stubble. She notices the old man is missing two teeth when he smiles.

Stella naively gets in and the old truck takes off with a roar.

"You're not from around here, are you, little lady? I can tell by how you talk. Where're you from?" the old man asks, gawking at Stella's slim form.

"No, I'm not from here. I'm from California, just visiting my grandparents for the summer," Stella admits. She doesn't realize her California accent is a giveaway.

"California? You're a mighty long way from home, little lady," says the old man with a gleam in his eye.

"Hey… there it is, the Blue Lantern… Hey, stop, you're passing it… Hey, get your grimy hands off of me…" Stella shouts out in panic.

The old man pulls Stella closer to him, grabbing her shoulder, reaching for her chest. Stella struggles to break free, hitting the old man with her bony fists, but to no avail. Her skinny arms have no muscles to propel any power.

Her eye catches the glimmer of the sun, shining on the silver key in the ignition. She grabs for it, turning the engine off, and pulling it out. With all her might, Stella throws the key out of the open window and the old truck coasts to a stop. She reaches for the door handle, but the old man seizes her by her arm and pulls her back to him.

"Why you little..."

Stella smells his sour beer breath, cringes, and screams. "You let go of me..." she shouts, kicking him in the groin as hard as she can, and the old man finally releases his grip. Stella grasps for the door handle and the truck door swings open, as she falls out of the truck, onto the road. Shaken from the hard fall, Stella slowly gets to her feet and sees the old man get out his truck.

Panic seizes her. She runs into the woods alongside the road, while the old man chases after her. She runs until she sees a thicket of trees and shrubs and ducks under the thorny bushes, hiding from sight. She can see the old man looking around, confused, then turning away, walking back to the road. She feels the brambles tearing at her flesh, the prickly vines tangling in her long hair, pulling at her ponytail. She waits in silence, listening, even though she wants to cry out in pain from the scraps and scratches. She hears the old man cursing in the distance, stomping about in his work boots. Finally, she hears the old Chevy pickup start up and drive away.

Stella crawls out from under the bushes and stands up. "Whew, that was a close call," she says out loud as she shivers at the thought of what may have happened. Brushing the dirt off her bare legs, then pulling the thorny vines from her hair, she notices her white cotton blouse is ripped and one of the buttons is missing. She sighs, "Yeah, never want to do that again."

Chapter 32

Walking slowly out of the forest, Stella sees a willowy young woman, with skin the color of warm caramel. Her long, curly black hair falls to her mid back and is tied back from her face with a yellow ribbon. She wears a simple dress of printed cotton that falls below her knees. Her hazel brown eyes squint as she walks up to Stella and asks, "Girl, what in the world happened to you? You look a mess."

Stella starts to sob and shake, as she tells the young woman about accepting a ride from an old man and fighting him off. "That old man had evil thoughts in his mind," Stella says as tears run down her cheeks, mingling with the dirt, giving her a ghoulish expression.

"Now, now, girl, don't you go crying on me. Here, here's a hankie to wipe those tears away from your pretty little face," the young woman says, pulling out a fine floral handkerchief from her pocket and handing it to Stella.

Stella takes the kerchief and wipes her face, then blows her nose into it.

"Uh… you can keep it," the young woman says when Stella offers to return it. They both laugh a little.

"Now, where y'all headin' on this hot humid day?"

"Well..." Stella says, sniffing back her stuffed-up nose. "I just thought I'd walk up to the Blue Lantern, to see my grandpa. He owns it, you see, and I can hang out there for a while."

"The Blue Lantern? You mean Mr. Pimperl is your grandpa? I didn't think Mr. Pimperl had any granddaughters," says the young woman, raising her eyebrows in surprise. "I know he has a mess of grandsons in these parts, but I don't know of any girls.

"Yep, he's my grandpa. I'm Stella. I'm from California. My mama's the oldest of seven children. Her mama didn't want her girls marrying farmers because it's such a hard life. She sent my mama to Chicago to work when she finished her schooling. She married my dad there but moved to California when the war broke out in Europe. California was the last state to draft for the war. But then war broke out in the Pacific and my dad was drafted anyways." Stella takes a deep breath, then continues. "I took the train out here to stay with my grandparents out on their farm for the summer."

"Well... glory be... I thought you did talk funny. No offense. I'm a headin' that way, so I'll walk with you. My name is Mazie. I live across the tracks. My granddady knew Mr. and Mrs. Pimperl way back when he lived in the woods. He'd bring Mrs. Pimperl her mail from Demco's. He had a big old horse he'd ride to town back then, at least that's what my grammy told me."

"What? Was his last name, Gelsinger?" Stella could not believe her ears.

"Why yes... how did you know?" Mazie questions, surprised by Stella's answer.

Stella ponders the connection of Mazie and Mr. Gelsinger. *Could her grandfather be the ghost that Grandma Margaret saw that hot summer night coming out of the woods, trying to tell her something when she fainted and struck her head?*

"Yep, my grammy loved that old man, Mr. Gelsinger. They had a child together." Mazie continues, wistfully thinking of the bittersweet ties to Gelsinger. "That child was my mama. My mama died birthin' me," Mazie reveals, casting her eyes downward and wringing her hands. Then perking up a bit, she says, "But my grammy takes good care of me and raised me like a daughter. She is the best as ever could be. Being a seamstress, she makes all my clothes from flour sacks, and from the scraps of fabrics, she sews beautiful, colorful quilts to keep me warm. And my, she can cook! She can fry up catfish she catches in the Tensaw, as flaky and good as you never tasted so good. And okra! Wow, her fried okra is the best. She'd read to me at night, before I'd go to sleep, books like *Tom Sawyer* and *Treasure Island*, that Mr. Gelsinger gave to her. And she makes sure I go to school every day, no matter what. She sure is good to me."

"What about your daddy, Mazie? What is he like?" Stella asks, curious to know since her grandmother raised her.

"Oh girl, my mama was thirteen years old when she got pregnant, too young to marry, even in Alabama. That Colored man who knocked her up in the cotton fields, just took off when he learned my mama was expectin' me. He was two times her age! Grammy tells me, 'Don't go messin' with any boys till you finish your schoolin'. No matter what they tell you, they's just plain trouble and get you in trouble.' Grammy'll whip me good, if I go sneakin' off with some boy and do the dance with no pants," Mazie answers with a little giggle.

"What's the dance with no pants?" Stella asks, puzzling over the phrase.

"You know, girl, when they put their private parts into your private parts and wiggle around, till they squirt." Mazie explains, and they both start laughing.

"Oh! Is that what they call 'sex', Mazie?"

Mazie just nods, her brown face turning red.

Changing the subject, Stella says, "Say, Mazie, my Grandma Margaret tells me your Grandpa Gelsinger was murdered and his ghost came back to haunt her. You hear about that?"

"Yes, indeed. My grammy told me she had just visited him and brought him some fried chicken and butter beans for his supper. They were having a bite to eat when there was a knock at the door of his shack. He told her to go out the back because folks don't think too kindly of white folks carrying on with us Creoles. So, she slipped out the back and hid in the forest. From the woods, she could hear a lot of yellin' and cursin'. Then

164

a single shot rang out. Bam! And she ran for her life. From a distance, she could see smoke and fire rising up from where Mr. Gelsinger's shack was in the woods. The smell of burnt pine trees filled the air and grey ash filled the sky hiding the full moon. She just kept on running till she got to her home across the tracks." Mazie takes in a deep breath, and lets a single tear fall from her hazel brown eye.

"I'm so sorry, Mazie. It must have been horrid for your grandmother. Did you know Mr. Gelsinger had money stashed under his house? My grandma tells me those men who came to his door that night, came to rob him. He wouldn't give up the money or tell them where the money was, so they shot him and burned down his house with him in it. Word is, they never found the money. Did you know about that?" Stella says, brushing the dirt off her clothes and straightening her appearance.

"Well actually, Mr. Gelsinger told my grammy, if anything ever happened to him, where he hid all his money. So, months later, when things settled down, my grammy was seven months along with his child, she snuck back over to where his shack had been and found three mason jars full of cash, under a layer of smashed tin cans covered with leaves. She told no one and used the money to start her seamstress business and pay the midwife who delivered the baby. She told me about it a few years ago. She's still saving some so when I finish school, I can go on to college, maybe be a nurse someday. Maybe…" Mazie says, her voice trailing off, thinking of all her grandmother went through.

"Well… I best be going to my grandpa's store," Stella says, tugging at her blouse.

"Here, Stella," she says, unfastening a safety pin on her hem, and handing it to Stella.

"Thanks." Stella accepts the pin and closes her wrinkled cotton blouse where the missing button once was.

"The Blue Lantern is not that far from here. We can walk there in about a fifteen-minutes," says Mazie. "I'll walk with you, just in case that creepy old man in the truck comes back."

"Thanks, Mazie. I'd like that," Stella says, and the two girls begin walking up the road talking of the differences between their two worlds.

Chapter 33

At the Blue Lantern, John Pimperl stands behind the counter. His thick greying hair is combed neatly to one side, his face is shaved clean carefully so as not to nick his cleft chin. He is wearing a white button-up shirt, long sleeves rolled up to the elbow. His black slacks are pressed with a crease down each leg, the cuff resting on heavy black work shoes. He is serving his friends, Frank Klasnich and Johnny Roley, each a cold bottle of Pabst Blue Ribbon beer and Johnny's son, Arnold, a frosty root beer from the cooler.

Mr. Frank is an old friend of John Pimperl, whose family settled on a sixty-acre piece of land close to the railroad tracks at the far end of Perdido in the 1920s. He is a big man, six-foot three, weighing over two hundred pounds in coveralls. He covers his fair hair with a wide brimmed hat to keep the sun off his face. Mr. Frank never married and enjoys a beer with friends at the Blue Lantern.

Johnny is short and wiry in coveralls and tee shirt, talking about the possible racial unrest in northern Alabama with Mr. Frank and John Pimperl. "Seems them Negros are causing a ruckus up in Montgomery and Birmingham," Johnny says in hushed tones.

"Yeah, I read something like that in the newspaper, but heck, we're as poor as they, and they picked the cotton same as us under the hot sun when I was a young'un. They no different from us, just their skin is darker." Mr. Frank speaks up, then takes a swig of his beer.

Arnold, wearing a striped tee shirt over his blue jeans, sits on a stool, sipping his root beer. He ignores the men's conversation, while reading his new Superman comic book.

When Stella and Mazie get to the Blue Lantern, Mazie waves good-bye to Stella and continues on her way.

The three men look up towards the door when they hear Stella's cheerful, "Hi, Grandpa!"

"Hi, Stella. Where's your Aunt Helen?" her grandfather asks, looking towards the door; he does not see Helen's blue Caddie outside.

"Oh, she's probably at home, or maybe with her boyfriend, Sam," Stella replies, shrugging her shoulders. She strolls in and sits on a stool next to Arnold and asks, "Can I have a soda pop, Grandpa?"

"Sure, sweet thing. You help yourself." Then glancing at her disheveled appearance, he asks, "How did ya get down here from the farm?"

"Oh… I was bored and I just started walking… then thought I'd walk to your store… I was walking along the highway to your store and…" Tears begin to well up in her eyes.

"What happened? Tell me!" John shouts so loud his voice frightens Stella, and she starts sobbing uncontrollably. Tears flow down her cheeks mixing with the dirt on her face.

Stella's grandfather waits patiently, staring at his frail granddaughter until she finally stops crying. Stella takes a deep breath and continues telling her story. "Well, this stranger stops his truck and offers me a ride to your store. And I'm thinking, that's a lucky break, save me some walking. Then he drives right past your store." Stella pauses and starts to break down again. "And then... grabs me by the shoulder and... then creeps me out by groping my chest! Grandpa, I fought him off, with all my might. I kicked and scratched. Then I grabbed the keys in the ignition and turned the truck off and threw those keys out the window. Grandpa, I grabbed hold of the door handle and the truck door opened and I jumped out, even with the truck still moving and rolled on the ground. That's why I'm so dirty. I ran into the forest and hid until I heard the truck leave."

Mr. Frank just shakes his head and mutters, "Good Lord almighty..."

Stella takes a deep breath, then lets it out slowly and gains her composure. "Grandpa, the girl with me, her name is Mazie. She was so kind to me..." Stella wipes her tears away with a paper towel from the counter.

John Pimperl gives his granddaughter a stern look and says, "Don't you ever do that again. Never..." he stutters slightly, "never accept a ride from a stranger."

Then John picks up the phone and dials home. The phone rings several times until Margaret answers. "Hello?"

John retells Margaret the events of the day. In his loud booming voice, he demands, "Get Helen on the phone!" yelling into the telephone.

Grandma Margaret hands the phone over to Helen. "Yes, Papa? What is it?" she says sweetly. When hearing what Stella did, Helen is shocked. "What? Oh, my Lord... I'll call Dotty in California right away. This is too much for me."

By the end of the day, Stella's mother, Dotty, buys a one-way train ticket from Bay Minette, Alabama to Los Angeles, California. She puts it in the mail, special delivery to her sister, Helen. In a few days, Stella is on her way back to California, just in time to start ninth grade at the local high school.

Chapter 34

Returning home to California, Stella witnesses the civil rights movement in Alabama play out on television over the next few years. She is horrified and appalled over the treatment of the Black people fighting for equal rights. The newspapers and television cameras capture the struggles and protests in Alabama and other southern states. However, it is Alabama that leads the way with non-violent marches led by Martin Luther King Jr.

The American civil rights movement starts in the mid-1950s. A major catalyst in the push for civil rights is in December 1955, when NAACP (National Association for the Advancement of Colored People) activist, Rosa Parks, refuses to give up her seat to a white man on a public bus.

Segregation is the legal and social system of separating citizens on the basis of race. KKK (Klu Klux Klan) members routinely disrupt civil rights meetings, including church services, with bomb threats. They suppress black citizens in Alabama and other southern states until they are dismantled during the civil rights movement in the 1950s and 1960s. Many civil rights protest marches take place in Birmingham at the steps of the 16th Street Baptist

Church, which is an important religious center for the city's black population and a routine meeting place for civil rights organizers.

On February 1,1960, seventeen-year-old Franklin McCain and three Black friends go to the Whites-only counter at Woolworths in Greensboro, North Carolina, and take a seat.

In 1963, President John F. Kennedy calls for the Civil Rights Act, which stops major forms of racial discrimination. The civil rights activism sparking the modern movement begins in the spring of that year. Activists in Birmingham, Alabama launch one of the most influential campaigns of the Civil Rights Movement: Project C, better known as the Birmingham Campaign. African American civil rights activists in Alabama start the Birmingham campaign, a series of sit-ins, boycotts and marches against segregation laws. The peaceful demonstrations are met with violence, teargas and police dogs. The events are the turning point in the civil rights movement.

On September 15, 1963, some two hundred church members are in the 16th Street Baptist Church—many attending Sunday school classes before the start of the eleven-a.m. service—when a bomb explodes on the church's east side, spraying mortar and bricks from the front of the church and caving in its interior walls. Most parishioners are able to evacuate the building as it fills with smoke, but the bodies of four young girls (fourteen-year-olds Addie Mae Collins, Cynthia

Wesley, and Carole Robertson and eleven-year-old Denise McNair) are found beneath the rubble in a basement restroom.

On 'Bloody Sunday', March 7, 1965, some six hundred civil rights marchers head east out of Selma on U.S. Route 80. They get only as far as the Edmund Pettus Bridge six blocks away, where state and local lawmen attack them with Billy clubs and teargas and drive them back into Selma. The civil rights march is meant to go from Selma to the capitol in Montgomery to protest the shooting death of activist, Jimmie Lee Jackson. On that day in Selma, Alabama, doctors and nurses work all night on more than one hundred patients, who are only accepted at one hospital, a Catholic mission facility in a black neighborhood. The most common injuries are lacerations and broken bones, but there are also fractured skulls and injuries secondary to teargas. The goal of the Selma march was to get voting rights legislation passed.

The Voting Rights Act of 1965 is the landmark piece of federal legislation in the United States that prohibits racial discrimination in voting. It is signed into law by President Lyndon B. Johnson during the height of the Civil Rights Movement on August 6, 1965, and Congress later amends the act five times to expand its protections.

***

In time, Stella learns the names of the great men who brought about change in the south. Martin Luther King Jr. (January 15, 1929 to April 4, 1968): the chairman of the Southern Christian Leadership Conference (SCLC) was a Baptist minister, activist, and the most famous leader of the Civil Rights Movement. King won the Nobel Peace Prize in 1964 and he posthumously wins the Presidential Medal of Freedom in 1977, nine years after his assassination in 1968. For his promotion of nonviolence and racial equality, King is considered a peacemaker and martyr by many people around the world. Martin Luther King, Jr. Day in the United States is established in his honor, and a memorial to him stands on the nation's National Mall today.

James Farmer (January 12, 1920 to July 9, 1999): In 1942 Farmer founds the Congress of Racial Equality or CORE, a pacifist organization dedicated to achieving racial harmony and equality through nonviolence. CORE stayed active in the Civil Rights Movement through the 1950s and 1960s. Farmer is awarded the Presidential Medal of Freedom in 1998, shortly before his death in 1999.

John Lewis, born February 21, 1940 becomes a leader in the Civil Rights Movement as president of the Student Non-Violent Coordinating Committee, (SNCC) and participates with other civil rights leaders such as Diane Nash, James Bevel, and Bernard Lafayette in the Nashville Student Movement (1959—62). John Lewis was one of the original thirteen Freedom Riders. Lewis represents SNCC with a speech at the August 28, 1963 March on Washington. Lewis has represented the Fifth District of Georgia in the United States House of Representatives since 1987, a district which includes almost all of Atlanta.

Philip Randolph (April 15, 1889 to May 16, 1979) becomes a socialist in the labor movement and the Civil Rights Movement. In 1925, Randolph organizes the Brotherhood of Sleeping Car Porters. This is the first serious effort to form a labor union for the employees of the Pullman Company, a major employer of African Americans.

Roy Wilkins (August 30, 1901 to September 8, 1981), a prominent civil rights activist in the United States from the 1930s to the 1970s, is named executive director of the (NAACP). He is an excellent, articulate spokesperson for the Civil Rights Movement. He participates in the March on Washington (1963), the Selma to Montgomery marches (1965), and the March Against Fear (1966).

Whitney Young (July 31, 1921 to March 11, 1971) spends most of his career working to end employment discrimination in the south and turning the National Urban League from a relatively passive civil rights organization into one that aggressively fought for justice.

Part III
Present

Chapter 35

More than fifty years have passed since the turbulent sixties. The ghosts who wear white bed sheets and pointy white hats are long gone from sight. It takes the assassination of a white president and a black religious leader to bring an end to segregation in the southern states. But the healing of the nation takes many decades. The old prejudice and bigotry die out with the older generation. A newer generation, more tolerant and more diverse, moves into the south. With education and opportunity, blacks are seen in every profession. They are seen in movies and on television, in businesses and in universities, in medicine and in science, in sports and in entertainment. No more are there signs in Alabama saying, 'White' and 'Colored' on water fountains and restrooms, separating the races. Instead, signs are posted prohibiting segregation and

discrimination in public offices and businesses in Alabama. The dream of Martin Luther King Jr. is coming true: "I have a dream that my four little children will one day live in a nation where they will not be judged by the color of their skin but by the content of their character."

Stella is much older now, living in California. When she looks in the mirror, she sees the lines and wrinkles in her pallid skin that age brings. She has stopped wearing makeup except for a peach-colored lip gloss but tints her colorless hair with copper-red henna and keeps it short. She has lost weight since the ravishes of breast cancer and the chemotherapy stole her once red hair. Even with the reconstructive surgery, she looks older than her years. Her gaunt body gives her a ghostly appearance. She now dresses in subdued, muted colors to hide her pathetic body and lack of confidence.

Her grandmother has passed away, as well as her own parents. Even her beloved Aunt Helen has passed. Stella recalls how her aunt took Stella under her wing that summer of 1960 in Alabama. Now the last of her mother's sisters, Elizabeth, at eighty-seven, has died. Her heart yearns to revisit the past and attend her auntie's funeral. It will be a chance to reconnect with the rest of her mother's family. It is late October, and the weather is cooling down in the south. The brutal heat of the summer is over.

Hearing the funeral is in three days, Stella makes a reservation for the next day and packs her small navy-blue suitcase. Memories rush through her head. She hasn't been back to Alabama for years. She feels anxious about the trip, wondering if any of her cousins will recognize her and how they will treat her. Will they accept her as part of the family or regard her as an outsider? She has only two girl cousins in Alabama and a dozen boy cousins, all much younger.

There is Dawn who is ten years younger than Stella. Dawn works for the water district as an accountant and wears dark, well-tailored suits or trendy casual clothes. Her hair is styled short and dyed a warm dark brown. Her makeup is perfect from her eyebrows to her lips. Dawn is all business, and you can tell by her stern brow and rigid posture.

Kay is the youngest of the cousins, at least by ten years. Her blonde hair is free and easy, cascading over her shoulders, parted at the side. She loves thickening up her lashes to bring out her aqua-green eyes. She is light-hearted, marrying a gentleman farmer, living near the Tensaw River on ten acres with lots of horses, cows and chickens.

Stella sighs out her nervousness, as she looks through her wardrobe to pick out the appropriate clothes for the trip. "Let's see… what do I have that's black? Not much," she says as she pulls out an outfit. "This little black rayon dress is too sexy for a funeral. Maybe with a black sweater over it," picking out a black polyester cardigan. "No, now it looks too dowdy… Well, I am an old lady now." She laughs to herself. Filling up her small suitcase with enough clothes to last a week, she snaps the clasps closed and sets it on the floor of her bedroom.

Mentally exhausted, Stella rubs her eyes. Her head is pounding from stress. It is such a long flight with two stops and hours of layovers. She really does not want to travel two thousand miles to see a dead body laid in the ground. But it is the last of her mothers' sisters. She feels the obligation of being there for whatever reason.

She shuffles to the kitchen for a glass of water and two aspirins. Standing over the sink, she opens the little bottle of pain reliever, shakes out two, pops them into her mouth and washes them down with water. "Ah... maybe I can sleep now," she mutters to herself.

With her headache fading, Stella wanders back to her bedroom, crawls into bed and turns off the light. In the dark room, she slips into a dream about cemeteries and spirits and the old man's ghost that haunts Dyas Creek.

Chapter 36

At dawn, Stella's alarm rings. She knows she must shower, dress, and drive to the airport by eight to catch her flight to Alabama. As she emerges from her shower and slips on her comfy pink sweatshirt and pants, her mind flashes back to the disturbing dream of the old man who was murdered so long ago. Her grandmother's ghost story has her on edge. She wishes her grandmother were still alive to answer questions about the crime. It seems as though, from what Stella has read about untimely deaths, the spirit of the deceased does not rest in peace, but instead roams around the place of death and looks for resolution of some unfortunate act.

Picking up her suitcase, Stella locks the front door behind her and hurries to her old blue Dodge Dart. She has had the old car since her college days and just recently put a new engine in it to prolong its life. Turning the key, the Dart comes to life with a roar and takes to the freeway like a racecar. Even though Stella is now a senior citizen, she feels like a teenager behind the wheel of her classic car.

The morning traffic picks up and now it is stop and go all the way to the airport. Stella parks in the overnight parking structure, locking her precious Dodge Dart, and walks to the terminal with her suitcase in tow with plenty of time to catch her flight.

There are lots of travelers going her way. The line to the check-in counter snakes down the hall. Stella waits patiently for her turn to check her bag and pick up her boarding pass. Time stands still as the line slowly moves with each customer.

"That'll be twenty-five dollars..." says the clerk at the counter.

"For what?" Stella questions the clerk.

"To check your bag, of course," the clerk says, frowning at Stella as if she is a child.

"When did you start charging for bags? I don't remember having to pay extra for checking my bags through," says Stella confused, shaking her head.

"Ah... about five years ago," the clerk says, rolling her eyes up towards the ceiling.

"Well then, I will just carry my suitcase on the plane. Okay?" Stella says, rather peeved to now pay for space in the luggage compartment. *Nothing is free anymore,* she thinks to herself, *not even the food on the flight.*

"Okay, then. Here's your boarding pass. Your flight leaves out of gate three. Have a pleasant trip," the clerk says with a forced smile.

"Thank you," Stella says right back with a forced smile.

Stella makes her way toward gate three, towing her ancient suitcase, when one of the wheels gets tangled up with something it picks up along the way. The stuck wheel wiggles, then turns the suitcase and tips over, springing the clasp. The contents spill out and scatter all over the terminal floor. Now Stella looks at her watch. Time is running out. Franticly, she drops to her hands and knees as she starts gathering her clothes, shoes and toiletries. Other travelers walk around her, viewing her dismay, as she stuffs her belongings back into her suitcase. But the clasp does not hold. The suitcase springs open again.

Don't cry, Stella tells herself. *Don't cry.*

A short middle-aged man with kind brown eyes comes up to Stella and asks, "Need some help, lady?"

"Why yes," Stella replies, trying not to cry. "My flight leaves in twenty minutes and my suitcase… the clasp on my suitcase just broke…" Stella takes a deep breath, "and… and it won't stay shut… I …"

"Don't cry. Here, lady try this," The stranger unbuckles his belt and wraps it around the suitcase and cinches it tight. "There, that should hold it."

"But your belt…" Stella pleads, "What about your belt. Won't you need it?"

"Don't worry. I have others. Just don't miss your flight," the stranger says.

"How can I ever thank you? You're too kind," Stella tells the kindhearted man.

"You just did. Now go!"

Then Stella hurries to the TSA line. There she waits her turn to take off her shoes, put all her belongings through the moving rollers that the agents scan. Now she must go through the metal detector to prove she has no bombs strapped on her person.

"Beep, beep, beep…"

"Ah, lady, step over here. I'm going to have to pat you down," says a heavy-set black woman in uniform, pulling Stella out of the line.

"What? I don't have any metal on me. See," Stella says, lifting up her sweatshirt to show her bare waist.

"Uh lady… that's not necessary. But regulations say we must pat you down if the buzzer sounds," says the TSA agent, approaching Stella.

"Hey! Don't touch me! Keep your hands away from me. I'm an old lady and I do not want anyone touching me," Stella says, pushing the woman in uniform away from her. Feelings of defensiveness and embarrassment flood over her since the removal of her cancerous breasts which have been replaced by two saline pouches.

"Hey! Are you targeting old people just because they won't fight back? I said, don't touch me!" Stella yells in a fit of rage.

"Now lady, calm down. If you don't let me pat you down, you are not getting on that airplane," says the TSA agent. Then she puts her phone to her ear and calls for assistance.

Two more agents show up to persuade Stella, who is now talking back and cursing in a high screechy voice. Other travelers gather around to watch the argument. Finally, Stella sees she is losing this battle. She allows the agents to escort her into a private room where the agent searches and pats her down, then sets her free. She grabs her suitcase with the man's belt around it with one hand and her shoes with the other and runs for Gate-3.

Stella is the last passenger to board the crowded airplane before it takes off. Walking down the aisle toward the back of the plane, she sees her seat number between two overweight travelers. She lifts open the overhead luggage compartment, only to find there is no room for her suitcase. The tall blond stewardess with the perfect makeup and hairdo strolls by saying, "Take your seat, ma'am. We are about to take off."

"But I can't get my bag in the overhead," Stella complains, holding back her tears. She feels totally defeated even before the plane takes off.

"You'll just have to stow your bag under the seat in front of you," replies the stewardess.

"Okay! Okay!" Stella snaps, as she stuffs her little suitcase under the seat. She thinks to herself, *Why in the world am I doing this? None of mother's family ever came to her funeral. And I don't really know these people. Well, my mother's sister did come to visit us in California, once. But what do I know of all the cousins who are all much younger than me. They don't know me from Adam. What can I say to them? I remember my Grandma Margaret and my Aunt Helen, but they are gone now. Gone to heaven. Their bones are lying in their graves now. Maybe they're ghosts now too, like that old man's ghost that Grandma Margaret saw so many years ago. Maybe their spirits haunt the woods, too.*

"Fasten your seatbelts, ladies and gentlemen. We're about to take off," the voice on the intercom announces.

Stella closes her eyes and feels the surge of the engines as the plane rumbles down the runway. Then the airplane lifts air bound, and she is on her way. "Oh well," she mutters under her breath, "too late now to change my mind."

Chapter 37

Landing in Mobile, Stella rents a car and drives to the funeral home in Bay Minette. She catches the tail end of the visitation, the viewing of the body. Many family members and friends are there to pay their respect. In a small, dimly lit room filled with flowers, they come up to the casket to look at her, say a few words, then turn away and talk to others in the room about her.

There she is, Stella says to herself, *Aunt Elizabeth, laid out in a pearl-white casket, in a red and white floral dress. Her short snowy-white hair is perfectly styled, her face looks tranquil and serene, as if she is sleeping. But we all know she is dead.*

Two of Stella's cousins come up to talk to her. "Hey, Stella, glad you could make it out here from California. Remember me? I am Dawn. I was just a kid the last time you came to Alabama. I'm Joey and David's sister," Dawn says, then hugs Stella briefly. She wears a black suit, white blouse, and black heels. She is perfectly dressed for the occasion.

"Thanks. Good to see you, too." Stella replies trying to figure out who is who.

Then Kay speaks up and says, "And I'm Kay. Remember me? I came out to California with my parents many years ago and stayed with your parents in

1982." Kay is dressed more casually than Dawn in black slacks and floral top.

"Oh, yes. I remember you, now. You were just a kid then, and we took you to… Disneyland." Stella says, her voice trailing.

Stella is exhausted from the long day of travel and can hardly keep her eyes open. She attempts to cover up a yawn, but Kay sees Stella's frailty and colorless complexion. Her eyelids are at half mast, set deep in dark circles around her eyes. Kay asks, "Where are you staying, Stella?"

"Oh, I don't know, Kay. I was going to get a motel room for the night and go to the funeral in the morning. I'm here for a whole week and I'm not sure what I'll be doing," Stella replies, feeling her eyes dampen from the tears she is holding back.

"Stella, stay with me! We have a big place on the river and my husband won't mind a bit. We have plenty of room. Stay with me," Kay pleads, touching Stella's arm tenderly.

"Well… are you sure I'm not intruding?" Stella hesitates.

"No, not at all. Your mama and daddy were so kind to us when we came out to California. We stayed with y'all, remember? You just come on home with me and we'll fix you right up. No problem," Kay insists.

"Yes, Stella, stay with Kay," Dawn agrees. "You look really tired out from the long flight from

California. We girls can get together tomorrow at the funeral and talk afterwards,"

"Well… okay," Stella says, feeling relief by her cousin's generous offer. She says her goodbyes to the family and friends at the funeral home. Getting into her rental car, she follows Kay out to her home by the Tensaw River. Kay leads Stella to a comfy guest room in the spacious farmhouse, where Stella settles in. Her heart is full, glad that she is accepted by her mother's family. She closes her eyes on the big fluffy four poster bed and dreams of her grandmother she stayed with so long ago.

Chapter 38

The next day is October 30th, the day of the funeral for Stella's aunt. Stella follows Kay and her husband back to the funeral home where everyone gathers in the small chapel full of flowers and the open casket. Dawn and her husband already have a seat close to the front and waves at Kay and Stella to join her. The chapel fills up quickly. Stella looks around, to see who else came to say their goodbyes to her Aunt Liz.

In the very last row sits a lady whose skin is the color of warm caramel. Her hair is styled short, with wavy strands of black and white framing her delicate face. On her petite body, she wears a long-sleeved dress with tiny red cardinals printed on the black fabric. She sits quietly with her weathered hands in her lap, her eyes looking down to avert the tears welling up.

The funeral service is a short one. The minister's eulogy is a list of the accomplishments of the dearly departed. There are no tears shed by Stella's distant relatives as they sit silent on the hard-wooden benches in the chapel.

The funeral service ends with the minister saying a prayer and then reciting *The Lord is my Shepherd..."*

Then the lady in the back row slips out the back of the chapel, dabbing her eyes with a small cotton handkerchief. She heads for her beige late model Lincoln, walking swiftly to avoid the crowd of mourners. Sitting behind the wheel, she waits until the others file out of the chapel and form a caravan to the cemetery. The pall bearers carry out the casket to the waiting black hearse. Slowly, the cars line up and the procession moves. The lady in the beige Lincoln pulls up behind the last car.

At the cemetery, the cars park and mourners gather around a three by six-foot hole dug in the ground with a blue canopy covering the hole. Stella sees the one black lady in the handful of white relatives standing a way back from the crowd.

Straining her eyes, Stella walks up to the lady and says, "Mazie, is that you?"

"That's my name. Do I know you?" the lady says, tilting her head to get a better look at Stella. Mazie stands a little distance from the other mourners, hoping to be discreet, but yet wishing to pay her respects to the patient she cared for, for many years, at the nursing home. Miss Liz, who they lay in the ground that day was so kind and generous to Mazie, always sharing candies and goodies her family brought her on special days. Mazie recalls the funny stories Miss Liz would tell, about her past, and they both would have a good laugh.

"I'm Stella, Miss Liz's niece. I was here in the Summer of 1960, staying with my Grandma Margaret. I was only fourteen years old. Do you remember me?" asks Stella, looking into her kind brown eyes, thinking back to that fateful day she tried to hitchhike to her grandfather's store, the Blue Lantern.

"Stella, the girl I found beside the road, all bruised up and dirty? You're that California girl, ain't you?"

"Yes! That's me. You sure helped me out that day," Stella says, her face flushing a little from embarrassment.

"Well, how are you, girl? Did you get home okay? Did your grandpa whip you for taking a ride from a stranger? That was extremely dangerous back then. Still is. You're lucky to be left unharmed, except for a few scrapes and scratches. These old men out here, they get liquored up and no tellin' what they'll try with a pretty young thing, like you were."

"I know now. Whew, that was a close call," Stella says, wiping her brow. "I went back to California, finished high school and then went on to college. I studied chemistry and went on to work for the police department in their crime lab, investigating forensic evidence. I was part of a team who figured out the cause of death in homicides. How about you, Mazie? What have you been doing all these years?

"I, too, finished high school and went to college. There was some old man who wanted to marry me that summer of 1960, but my grammy said, 'No way! Not my granddaughter.' She had a little extra money she put away, and I went on to nursing school and became a registered nurse. I worked for the convalescent home in town for many years. I knew your auntie there. She was one of my favorite patients. She was so nice to me. Never said a mean word to me," Mazie says, lowering her eyes to hide her sadness. "I come to pay my respects to that kind lady." She reaches into her handbag and retrieves a pink and white flowered hankie made of fine thin cotton. Mazie dabs her eyes to soak up the tears before they fall.

Now the pall bearers lower the casket into the ground and a few words are spoken, breaking the stillness of the day. Then friends and relatives start chatting with one another. Stella sees her cousins, Kay, and Dawn, standing together talking.

"Come on, Mazie. I want you to meet my cousins," Stella says, pulling on her arm.

"Oh no, that's your family," Mazie says slightly embarrassed. She remembers how it was back when she was a child. The Colored folk didn't mix with the White folk. It just wasn't done.

"Oh, come on, I insist. One of my cousins built her home where the old farm and barn was. Maybe she knows where your Grandpa Gelsinger had a home out in the woods…" Stella sighs, then changes the subject. "Hey Mazie, maybe his treasure is still there. Did you ever find the money?"

"No. My grammy only found a couple of jars of silver coins after the house was burnt down to the ground by those robbers. She was always afraid to go back. It was dangerous to be out after dark, especially with the Klan roaming around at night." Mazie says with a shudder.

"Tomorrow is Halloween, maybe we could investigate tomorrow. Let's talk to my cousins about it. I am sure they would be game for an adventure. Come on!" Stella insists.

Stella persuades Mazie to walk over and meet Dawn and Kay. Stella tells her cousins Mazie's grandmother was Gelsinger's girlfriend and that her mother was his child. Mazie's mother was raped at fourteen and died in childbirth. Mazie was that child.

"Gelsinger? You're Gelsinger's granddaughter?" Dawn speaks up in surprise. "Why, I know where Gelsinger's shack was. It is way in the forest, way back behind the old corn field, behind our house where the old barn once was. I know the way. I can lead you there, no problem. There's talk about the old man hiding his money under his house."

"Well, let's meet at Dawn's house to search for the old man's shack and search for the jars of money under what is left of his house. Who knows what we might find," says Stella.

"If we find anything of value, it should go to Mazie. She deserves it. She is his kin," Dawn says with a nod to Mazie.

"Yes, I agree," Kay says with a wise smile. "We girls will help you find Gelsinger's treasure if it's there. Let's meet tomorrow night at five."

"I'll try to get off work early," Dawn says, looking at her watch. "That will give us a couple of hours before dark. Everyone, bring flashlights."

"Then it's settled, the four of us will meet at Dawn's house at five," Stella says. Then as an afterthought, "Maybe since it is Halloween night, we could have a séance and call on Gelsinger's spirit to tell us where the treasure is hidden. He tried to tell Grandma Margaret when he was killed. Maybe he will tell us," Stella suggests. "You never know."

The four ladies look at each other feeling a little nervous, when Mazie speaks up and says, "That's a good idea. My grammy told me how to do it. How to call on the dead. She's part Creole, ya know. And since I'm his granddaughter, he may answer to me."

"Well... okay then... It's a date," Stella says to the other three ladies. Then she strolls over to her auntie's grave and says, "Rest in peace, dear Auntie. I'll see you when I get to heaven," then leaves the cemetery with the others.

Chapter 39

The next evening Stella drives out to Dawn's house. Driving through a canopy of tall trees at the edge of the forest to the end of Pimperl Road, Stella recalls the old farmhouse she stayed in the summer of 1960, now gone. Gone as well is the old barn, where her Aunt Helen taught her how to milk Old Betsy, the cow. Her mind floods with memories of warm days sitting on the wooden swing hanging on chains from the ceiling of the screened in porch. She remembers looking up at the sky, the amazing starry nights, and seeing bats whizzing by, eating mosquitos frantically flying about. The songs of the forest critters and the sweetness of the air from the tall pines, tell Stella she is back in her 'Sweet home Alabama'.

She drives up to the house and sees Mazie step out of her car, her greying, deep wavy hair replacing her long black curls of long ago. Her skin is still smooth and lustrous, brown, not black. Her once thin willowy body, is now strong and sturdy from years of working in the fields as a young woman, but now from nursing and caring for the elderly. Mazie walks slowly to Dawn's house, tired of caring for others, but continues to work to supplement her husband's wages. Her three children are now grown and working well paid jobs. However,

Mazie cares for her grandchildren in the day, even though she works a twelve-hour shift, three nights a week.

"Hey, Mazie," Stella shouts out. "You doin' all right?" She walks up to Mazie, giving her a warm hug.

"Why yes, Miss Stella. You doin' all right?" Mazie says and hugs back.

"Fine as a silver dime," Stella answers back with a nod and a smile. "I see Kay is already here," she says, as she knocks briskly on the door.

Kay comes to the door and opens it saying, "Come on in. Dawn is changing her work clothes. She thought jeans and boots will be better for walking through the bush than her dress and high heels." They all laugh at the thought.

Dawn soon appears. She is ready for anything. She has on rugged jeans and heavy leather boots. In one hand she has a flashlight and the other her phone with a GPS application. "Y'all ready, ladies? Got your flashlights with new batteries?

They all nod.

"Then, let's go. I have a couple of shovels outside we can bring with us," Dawn says, as they walk out the door.

They pick up the shovels and Dawn leads the way toward the back of her property on a footpath, through an old cornfield, now overgrown with weeds. The sun is setting in the west, casting long shadows beside them.

Soon they get to the forest of tall pines, leaves and pine straw litter the ground.

"I thought Gelsinger's shack was right around here," Dawn says searching the area at twilight with the beam of her flashlight.

"Let's stop here and try to call up old Gelsinger's spirit with a séance," Mazie says, feeling a strong emotional pull from the area. "Everyone, hold hands and form a circle."

The others say nothing and grab each other's hands. Stella feels a creepiness raising the hair on her arms, making her skin tingle. She looks around but sees nothing strange.

Mazie starts to speak, "Oh Mr. Gelsinger… if your spirit can hear me… I am your granddaughter… I know of your pain… your untimely death… I have come with Margaret Pimperl's three granddaughters. I have come to hear what you tried to tell Margaret so long ago. Mr. Gelsinger… Come forward… speak to us… speak to us that we may right a wrong and let your spirit rest in peace. Come, Mr. Gelsinger…"

Suddenly, a shadow appears out of the woods, moving closer. The women start to shiver in the warm night and hold on tighter to each other's hands. As the apparition comes closer, it appears to be an old man, with a long white beard, burnt black as charcoal, his coveralls in shreds. He opens his mouth, but nothing comes out. Instead, Mazie goes into a trance and her voice changes to the gravelly hoarse voice of an old man.

His words come out of Mazie's mouth. *"Granddaughters of Margaret... hear me... I have hidden my money away... no one will find it except you. Follow me... I will show you... Follow me."*

The four granddaughters stare at each other in shock. The ghost glides past the women and bravely, still holding onto each other's hands, they follow the ghost. He stops over a thick pile of decomposing tree bark, leaves and pine needles, then disappears. There seems to be something that looks like a small white stick, a finger, peeking out of the pile of leaves.

Stella lets go of Kay's hand, then carefully brushes the debris away, while the others shine their flashlights on the area. Soon Gelsinger's full skeletal remains are exposed. The ladies gasp at the white bones with a bullet hole through the chest area, shattering the ribcage. The skeleton's boney finger points in a southernly direction. More debris is brushed away until a layer of flattened tin cans is exposed. One by one, the ladies remove the tin cans until, to their astonishment, the rusty tops of metal mason jars are uncovered.

Chapter 40

One by one, twenty-seven mason jars are lifted out of the earth in the woods that night. The four ladies are shocked by what they see. They can hardly believe their eyes. Each jar is full to the top with old gold and silver coins, and dollar bills.

"Yippee! Mazie, you're rich!" shouts Kay, jumping up and down in the dark night.

"Quite down, Kay. Someone may be watching," Dawn says glancing around nervously.

"Can it be real, all this money here, all this time?" Mazie asks, doubtful of what she sees. "Pinch me. Maybe I'm dreamin'."

"We can't all be dreaming," Stella says, pinching Mazie and laughing when Mazie pinches her back.

"Well, there is one way to find out if it's all real," sighs Mazie. "Let's open the jars and see what's in them." She takes off her sweater and lays it on the ground. Then she opens one of the mason jars and dumps the contents onto her sweater. The silver dimes, quarters and dollars and a few gold pieces are all minted in the early 1900s. The dollar bills, ones, fives, tens and twenties are printed before 1910 and have 'Silver Certificate' at the top, instead of 'Federal Reserve

Note'. Mazie picks up one of the many silver dollars and bites down on it. "Ouch! Darn it! I chipped a tooth."

"It's real, all right." Stella says with a sigh of relief.

"Yippee!" Kay shouts out again.

"Thank you, Grandpa Gelsinger. Thank you, God," Mazie humbly prays. "Now I can finally retire and take it easy. And I can give Grandpa Gelsinger a proper burial and gravestone."

Dawn calls her husband on her cellphone and asks him, "Hey, honey, can ya come pick us up in the woods? We're down in the hollow, behind the old corn field. And Sweety, can ya bring some cardboard boxes with you? Yes, boxes, bring enough to carry a couple dozen mason jars... That's right!"

Mazie looks over at the three granddaughters of Margaret and sighs, "Without you three, that money would've laid in that ground forever. I want you each to take a jar of money for all your help. I insist."

"Oh, Mazie, you don't have to," Stella protests.

"Didn't you hear me, girl? I insist!" Mazie fires back.

"Okay, Mazie. Thank you so much." Stella responds and chooses one of the mason jars.

"Thanks, Mazie. God bless you." Kay and Dawn reply and each picks a jar of money.

Dawn's husband arrives with his truck and they load up all the jars into the cardboard boxes, as Mazie gathers up her sweater holding the contents of one jar of money.

When they get back to Dawn's house, Mazie calls her husband. "Jack, it's me, Mazie. I'm over at the old Pimperl farm. Come on down here and call our Uncle Joe. Bring him down here with you. We've found my Grandpa Gelsinger... Yes, after all these years... Yes, we also found the money he buried... Yes, behind the old Pimperl farm... Tell Uncle Joe to come on down here, and pick up old Grandpa Gelsinger's bones for burial... See you soon."

***

In the days that follow, Mazie and Stella pick out a proper casket for Gelsinger's remains.

The three cousins attend Gelsinger's funeral with all of Mazie's family and friends. They are the only white women there in the Negro cemetery across the railroad tracks.

Mazie bows her head by the gravesite and says, "Rest in peace, dear Grandfather... And thanks for the money."

And he did rest in peace, never to haunt the woods again.

THE END

March 15, 2020